RAVE REVIEWS FOR DON FLYNN'S
MURDER ISN'T ENOUGH

"New York *Daily News* reporter Flynn's first novel
... rings with authenticity!"   — *Publishers Weekly*

"GOOD WRITING, A GOOD PLOT, AND A VERY
GOOD READ ... Fortunately for suspense story fans,
both Flynn and his publishers have promised he will
write others to follow this one!"

— *Houston Chronicle*

"ENGAGING . . . Flynn's smooth narrative is en-
hanced by his mastery of the setting. He knows New
York and its neighborhoods, and he's especially well
versed in what it's like in a courthouse pressroom."

— *Newsday*

"WELL-PACED . . . CLEVER . . . A VERY
DELIGHTFUL, DOWN-TO-EARTH SERIES
CHARACTER."   — *Mystery Loves Company*

"A PLOT THAT HURDLES FROM SHOCK TO
SHOCK . . . FITZGERALD'S ASKEW SENSE OF
HUMOR MAKES THIS A STANDOUT!"

— *Booklist*

"LIVELY."   — *Kirkus*

Jove Books by Don Flynn

MURDER ISN'T ENOUGH

Watch for

MURDER ON THE HUDSON
coming in January!

DON FLYNN

MURDER ISN'T ENOUGH

JOVE BOOKS, NEW YORK

For Char,
the woman who . . .

All the characters and events portrayed in
this story are fictitious.

This Jove book contains the complete
text of the original hardcover edition.

MURDER ISN'T ENOUGH

A Jove Book / published by arrangement with
Walker and Company

PRINTING HISTORY
Walker edition published 1983
Published simultaneously in Canada by John Wiley & Sons Canada,
Limited, Rexdale, Ontario
Jove edition / October 1989

ISBN: 0-515-10151-6

Jove Books are published by The Berkley Publishing Group,
200 Madison Avenue, New York, New York 10016.
The name "JOVE" and the "J" logo
are trademarks belonging to Jove Publications, Inc.

PRINTED IN THE UNITED STATES OF AMERICA

10 9 8 7 6 5 4 3 2 1

1.

"WILLINGLY give yourself up to Clotho, allowing her to spin your thread into whatever she pleases," advises Marcus Aurelius. The maxims of the wise ancient Roman emperor slipped into my mind that morning in the New York *Daily Tribune* city room when the obituary jumped out at me. Clotho had snipped the mortal thread of one Sandy Pearl, legman.

You probably don't even know what a legman is. It's a more or less illiterate newspaper reporter. He can read, but he can't write; or at least not well enough for the columns of *The Daily Tribune*. Sanford Pearl was a legman for *The Daily Tribune*—and a good one—until some drunk or young punk ("person or persons unknown" the police report said) came screeching along Mulberry Street behind the Manhattan Criminal Court Building in a dark green Ford Galaxy and flung him against the iron fence bordering the Chinatown playground. The report said he was drunk when he walked out of Mazza's Cafe, and that he stepped in front of the Galaxy. I hope he was drunk enough not to know what hit him.

Sandy Pearl's obit wasn't much. A fat paragraph. Ben Hecht once wrote about reporters:

> We know each other's daydreams,
> And the hopes that come to grief.
> For we write each other's obits,
> And they're godalmighty brief.

I could have written a few thousand irreverent words about Sandy from our benighted days on the lobster trick. I used to joke that I created Sanford Pearl, and in a sense I did.

In those days, Sandy's fertile mind would come up with

5

an imaginative story and I would write it with suitable flair. Sandy would hang around to make sure his name was on the story along with mine:

By Sanford Pearl and Edward Fitzgerald

"How come your name comes second when you're the one who wrote the story?" he would ask.

"Because when the inevitable libel suit is filed on the basis of your drivel, I want your name out front," I would tell him.

"Fitz!"

It was Ironhead Matthews, the city editor, and he informed me that I had just inherited Sandy Pearl's job. I looked at him in some confusion. "Me?"

"You," said Ironhead. And just like that my days as a rewriteman at *The Trib* were over. All of a sudden, I was the reporter at the Manhattan State Supreme Court Building. Clotho, whom the Romans believed was the Fate that spun our thread of life, had turned her attention to me, it seemed. To me, the new job was a demotion. For years, the rewriteman was king in New York, especially at *The Trib*. But the electronic revolution had come, and now they needed writing reporters instead of legmen. It was a pain in the ass. I'd gotten comfortable in the office.

"You're turning into a hothouse plant. Go out and see if the city's still there," said Ironhead, who got his nickname as a young reporter when he survived being slugged by a nightstick while covering a riot.

The city was still there, all right. It's amazing what a place New York City is. I'd been a rewriteman for several years, but I didn't really know where the Manhattan State Supreme Court Building was. Foley Square. For god's sake, I didn't know where Foley Square was.

I remember this million dollar TV anchorman who was imported from California and started talking about the Metropolitan Museum of Art being in midtown. That's what happens when you're a hothouse plant for too long. You lose your perspective, not to mention your sense of geography.

The Manhattan State Supreme Court Building is a neo-classic treasure built in the days when courthouses were supposed to have awesome grandeur. They were designed to overwhelm you with the august power of The Law, and the Manhattan State Supreme Court Building is awesome. It has sweeping stone steps in front that are a block long and were obviously designed in Hollywood. A row of huge stone pillars rise two stories and on top of them, in gigantic bas relief letters, is a motto: The True Administration of Justice is the Firmest Pillar of Good Government.

But Sandy Pearl's office—my office now—made up for it. It was a musty, dimly-lit room off the lobby and my heart sank at the sight of it. It was right out of *The Front Page*. Sandy Pearl would never have gotten the Good Housekeeping seal of approval for his desk, either. It was littered with newspapers, scraps of paper with hastily scrawled notes on them, clippings, old coffee containers. On the wall was a large calendar showing the whole year at a glance. The previous year's calendar, a bigger one, was behind it, with a third year's behind that. There was nothing to mark this particular office as Sandy's—no pictures of his wife, for instance. Press rooms are like that. The occupant knows he's only passing through, even though he may have the office for 20 years.

There were several metal lockers along the wall, all of them empty except for pairs of rubbers and an umbrella with bent ribs.

Bobby, the head copy boy, had given me a spare key to the desk. I was able to get at the ancient upright Underwood typewriter that had been moldering away since whoever pre-

7

ceded Sandy Pearl put it there. The typewriter ribbon was a few shreds of black silk, the dust was undisturbed, and the gummy crud was everywhere. I hit a key on the typewriter and the letter arm rose and stuck.

The inside of the desk drawer, unlike the top, was a model of neatness. Everything was laid out more or less exactly. It struck me that Sandy was like that. His hair was usually mussed and his clothes rumpled, but the brain inside was clear and relatively uncluttered.

There wasn't much inside the desk. A few paperback books, some old court papers, the yellowing opening chapter of a novel or, maybe, a fanciful autobiography. There was a smattering of matchbooks from some pretty fancy singles bars—Maxwell's Plum, Dionysos, even one from Elaine's. There was a yellow, legal-sized pad of paper, on which Sandy had written "2381." The number was underlined three times and had two exclamation points after it.

There wasn't much else except a stack of empty white envelopes that had been torn open. They appeared to be letters that had arrived and had been opened, except that there was no address and no stamp. If they were letters, they had been hand delivered.

Then I noticed one envelope that was still sealed. I don't know why I opened it, but I did, without a thought. It wasn't addressed and it had no stamp, so I opened it. I wonder what might have happened if I'd just turned it over to Marcia, Sandy Pearl's wife? Inside the envelope was another, smaller white envelope, also without an address or marking of any kind. And inside the second white envelope were five $100 bills.

I don't know what the hell I expected to find, but those $100 bills immediately made me wonder what was going on. Sandy Pearl wasn't the kind of guy who had $100 bills. Who was? I started thinking about that, and I realized that he wasn't the kind of guy who got drunk, either. He was really a very timid little guy who watched his money and drank Seven-Up. Or at least, he was when I knew him on the midnight shift. I hadn't actually seen Sandy, except walking through the *Trib* city room once in a while, in several years.

A quick examination of the other plain white envelopes showed that each of them also had a second, smaller envelope inside. All had been torn open. The one thing in my dismal little office I could lock was the desk drawer. I shoved the envelopes—including the one with the $100 bills—into it and locked it.

I leaned back in the creaky swivel chair and lit a Tiparillo.

People sometimes ask how a reporter gets onto a story. Well, that's how. Something doesn't wash. When a City Hall clerk drives a Cadillac and dines out at "21," you start wondering. You don't expect to see a nun in a topless go-go joint, and you don't expect the Sanford Pearls of this world to walk around with what Damon Runyon used to call "large, coarse bills."

Sandy Pearl with $100 bills? No way.

My first impulse was to call the police and tell them about the $100 bills. But I was afraid the cops, being cops, would jump to conclusions. Large bills, and indications that there had been a stream of other large bills, might lead them to jump to the same conclusions that I was jumping to. What I had was a suspicion that something wasn't kosher. The best reason I had for going to the cops was also the best reason I had not to.

Foley Square is the hub of the court system in lower Manhattan. Next to the State Supreme Court is the massive United States Federal Courthouse of the Southern District of New York. It has Hollywood-type steps and pillars, too. If an I.C.B.M. ever demolishes Manhattan, future visitors will stumble upon Foley Square and think they've found the equivalent of the Roman Forum.

Next to the U.S. District Courthouse is a Disney Yellow Brick Road complex where they've thrown up the new mustard-colored Police Headquarters and the new Federal Detention Center. The whole thing has passageways four floors up connecting one building to the other and it looks like some modern version of the Bastille or Château D'If. I wandered through this maze until I found the new Police Headquarters, and then dropped into the press room to see Dubbs Brewer, our dapper police reporter *extraordinaire*. I found him in a modern, airy cubicle that was all steel furniture and pastel walls.

"Hey, Fitz," Dubbs smiled. "How'd they ever blast you out of the city room?"

"Dubbs!" I greeted him. He was a good example of the way people fit the image others have of them. Dubbs's suit was Robert Hall conservative, complete with vest, but his hat and his manner were 1940's Humphrey Bogart. Dubbs lived up to his hat and manner and ignored the suit. He had a regular table at P. J. Clarke's—he really did—and he talked like a detective out of *Laura*. We shot the bull for a few minutes and I told him that since Foley Square was my new address I wanted to have a look around.

"That was tough about Sandy Pearl," I finally said.

"Yeah," he said.

"Did you see the accident report?" I asked Dubbs.

"Did I see the accident report? Yeah. Hit-and-run. Accidental death. By person or persons unknown."

"How can it be accidental if it was hit-and-run?"

"How can it be accidental?" Dubbs echoed. "Simple. They got no reason to think it wasn't accidental."

"The driver left the scene. Doesn't that make it criminal?"

"Yeah. You could say that."

"Listen, Dubbs," I said. "You ever go out bouncing with Sandy?"

"Did I ever go out bouncing with Sandy?"

"Did you ever see him at P. J. Clarke's?"

Dubbs glared at me as though I'd insulted him. "Naw. He didn't go to class places. He didn't go out much at all, that I know of."

"How about the sauce? Was he hitting the booze?"

"How about the sauce?" dittoed Dubbs. "Naw. He wasn't much of a drinker."

That's what I'd always thought. "The accident report said he was drunk when he walked in front of that car," I said.

"I thought that was kind of funny, too," Dubbs said. "I guess he just tied one on that night."

"Who's investigating the case?" I asked.

"Who's investigating the case?" said Dubbs. "Nobody. There's nothing much to investigate."

We talked about my new assignment a little, and Dubbs pumped me for news of office gossip, and then I started to leave.

"Something bugging you about Sandy?" Dubbs asked.

"Yeah."

"What?"

"Well, dammit, Dubbs, he didn't drink or go out. It's like the cheerleader who gets laid one time and gets knocked up."

"You got to have something more than that," Dubbs said. "Have you?"

I wasn't ready to tell him about the five $100 bills. Dubbs wasn't a police reporter for nothing.

When I knew Sandy on the lobster shift, he was such an amateurish drinker that the boys called him "Candy Ass." I told Dubbs that.

"They still call him that," said Dubbs. "Or they used to."

I left the Bastille and came out onto the plaza that con-

11

nects St. Andrews Church and the immense Municipal Building, and I sort of half-noticed it all. It was really quite impressive, but I couldn't get my mind off Sanford Pearl, the Candy Ass drinker who just happened to tie one on the night he was totaled by a hit-and-run driver. That's the way it is with a story. It gnaws at you. You have to find those loose ends. Because if there was something fishy about Sandy's death, somebody was getting away with it.

That's what always bugged me, anyway. The politicians are looting the city. But that's not what bothered me so much. What bothered me was that they were getting away with it. It's my goddam middle-class background. I always had the feeling that criminals eventually got caught, that they went to trial and were convicted if guilty. It was inevitable. Criminals went to prison.

At the end of the day, I was half-way down the Hollywood stairs when I remembered the $100 bills and the envelope in the desk. I went back and got them and put them in my wallet. It was a nice, powerful feeling to have those big ones in my pocket. What the hell—I'm not the kind of guy who walks around with large, coarse bills, either.

By the time I got home to East 82nd Street that night, I was anxious to tell Madilyn all about it. She was home when I called, for once, and I jumped right into an account of it. Maddy always loved hearing about the usually nutty stuff going on at *The Trib*, and I thought she'd get a kick out of a little real mystery for a change.

"When are you coming?" I asked, and told her I'd actually gotten a bookcase and was making some sort of order out of chaos. "You're going to love this place so much you'll forget all about Chicago."

You know how it is when you're in a conversation with someone you're in tune with, and you alternate little signals back and forth so it's all one continuous communications beam, like a landing beam that a jet liner comes in on, alternating a beep with a beep from Air Traffic Control so that one steady hum is maintained? That's the way it had been with Maddy and me since we'd met on her trip to New York. We knew then that it was only a matter of time until she came to the Big Apple and moved in with me on East 82nd Street.

"Listen," I went on. "Just before you head for O'Hare to get the plane, go by Due's and pick up a sausage pizza, will you? There just ain't no pizza like Due's in New York. I freely admit we're deficient in that regard."

"Fitz . . . listen . . ."

Right away, I could hear something in her voice. The complementary beam wasn't coming in.

"Fitz, I don't know how to say this . . ."

2.

MY competition at the courthouse turned out to be a Prussian colonel, complete with bristling mustache, named Jed Starnes, of the *New York Times*, and a leprechaun named Harry Reeves, of the *New York Post*. Other assorted ink-stained wretches showed up from time to time when a good story broke, but we were the three regulars. Reeves had been covering State Supreme Court for about a hundred years and was the dean of our little press corps. He showed me around the building—Special Term Part 2, where show cause orders were issued, Special Term Part 1, where they were argued before a judge, the county clerk's office, where new cases were indexed. It was a complex maze, learned only through months, or even years, of patient accumulation.

My musty cubbyhole seemed less drab that second day. I stopped by the office and picked up a Texas Instruments Silent 700 electronic typewriter that enabled me to write stories and then send them into the *Tribune* typesetting system on the phone.

Since Harry Reeves had given me a Cook's tour of the building, I took him to lunch. He picked the spot, though— Giambone's, an Italian restaurant across the park behind the Criminal Court Building on Mulberry Street.

Giambone's is to the Foley Square crowd what the Algonquin Roundtable must have been to George S. Kaufman and the old *New Yorker* bunch. At lunchtime, it fills up with lawyers, judges, politicians, an occasional lurid defendant, and, of course, the press. Reeves, because of his long tenure, had a press table near the front. Anybody with a good story would stop by Reeves's table. A stream of lawyers and

14

judges came by. Reeves introduced me, in his own leprechaunish way, as "Fitzboggen of *The Trib*."

"Fitz-who?" I made the mistake of asking.

"All you left-footed Irishers are out of the peat bogs."

"Oh."

It was quite a lunch. There was Justice Liff, who sentenced murderers to death even though there was no death penalty. There was the Manhattan district leader, who named judges the way other people name kittens—for a going rate of $100,000 per nomination. There was the highest paid criminal lawyer in New York, Bernard W. Weinberg, who boasted that he never lost a case if the fee were paid in advance. I think I even saw William Kunstler with his House of Lords hairdo.

Bernard W. Weinberg, a miniature Jew who spoke just enough Gaelic to startle you, stopped by and smiled a crinkly-eyed smile from a parchment-paper face.

"*Cead mile failte*," said Weinberg, handing me a piece of hard candy wrapped in cellophane. It meant "a hundred thousand welcomes" in Gaelic, and he seemed pleased to explain it to a guy with an Irish name like mine.

"Don't feel bad," he smiled. "Lord Briscoe was equally surprised." Lord Briscoe was once the Jewish Lord Mayor of Dublin, as Weinberg was quick to point out.

"He's got fifty lawyers working for him," Reeves said when Weinberg had moved on.

Well, I don't know who all I met that day. They came in waves, and Reeves was always careful to let the word out that a new *Daily Tribune* reporter was covering State Supreme Court. He did it with consummate protocol.

"Judge Starke, this is Fitzboggen of *The Trib*."

Reeves wasn't one to let you get the big head. It wasn't long before I was calling him, with due reverence, "a pain in the grumper." I tried to question him about Sandy Pearl.

"What the hell," said Reeves. "He's dead."

What I wanted to know, of course, was whether Sandy was a big spender, whether he had become a sport and a heavy drinker. I especially wanted to have some explanation for that money.

"Will you listen to me?" snorted Reeves. "Sandy Pearl wouldn't spend a dime! He wouldn't come here for lunch. He had fishhooks in his pockets."

"Did he drink?"

"Aw, what the hell are you talking about?" Reeves looked at me with disgust. "For Chris' sake, he'd suck on one lousy beer for an hour. Like you."

I had been sucking on one beer. Reeves drank "bombs" —martinis.

"He never went anywhere. He never did anything. He never told anybody anything."

"Would you say he was secretive?"

"Secretive? He used to lock the goddam door to make a phone call."

Well, Reeves insisted on buying another round—a Schaefer for me and a "bomb" for him—and then the district leader sent over another round.

I explained the whole thing to Reeves—except about the five $100 bills—and asked him how come Sandy Pearl was drinking on Mulberry Street at 11 o'clock on a Wednesday night if he was a candy ass who never went anywhere and never did anything?

"How come he wasn't at home in Larchmont with his wife?"

"How'd you ever become a reporter? How's that add up to anything at all?"

I wasn't going to get anywhere without telling him about the $100 bills. But the minute I told him that, it would become a story, and Sandy Pearl would have some questions to answer. And he wasn't exactly in a position to do that.

Justice Herbert Foley, a white-haired, venerable old jurist with about 40 years on the bench, stopped by to inquire after our health. He had been, consecutively, magistrate, judge of General Sessions, Supreme Court justice, and was currently one of two New York county surrogates. He walked into the back of Giambone's to join Weinberg, who was still speaking Gaelic.

The gentleman was balding and smiling and there was a pixie gleam in his eye. "Judge Nacht," said Reeves, "meet Fitzboggen."

Judge Nacht sat down and pulled out a deck of cards. "Pick a card, any card," he said.

Well, what the hell, the whole damned idea of Sandy Pearl disappeared in the conviviality of Giambone's. It seemed more and more ridiculous when measured against the reality of my new beat. Besides, Judge Nacht's magic tricks required our full attention.

It wasn't until we left the place that I happened to glance down Mulberry Street and saw Mazza's Cafe that I thought of it again. I realized I was right on the spot where it had happened. There, across Mulberry Street, was the Chinatown playground. There was the iron fence.

"That's Mazza's," I said.

"You don't want to go there," said Reeves. "Scotch is two bucks a shot."

"That's where Sandy Pearl was that night."

Reeves looked at me. "For Chris' sake."

"I'll see you later," I told him, and walked down Mulberry Street. Reeves was calling me a Boy Scout. At that point on Mulberry Street, the street is barely wide enough for a car to get through. They were parked at both curbs, and it was a narrow street. Whoever came speeding along Mulberry Street had to have known it pretty well, I thought.

The higher price of Scotch wasn't all that evident in the decor. There was a small bar in front, and tables upstairs and downstairs. There was also a fine, big azure mural on the wall behind the bar. Looked like the Venetian Grand Canal. I ordered a Schaefer, lit up a Tiparillo, and introduced myself.

"Ed Fitzgerald, *Daily Trib*."

Hank Mazza, dark and wiry and about 35, gave me a look somewhere between hostility and curiosity.

"I'm replacing Sandy Pearl."

Hank put a shot glass on the bar and poured a slug of Cutty Sark. He lit a Benson & Hedges menthol cigarette.

"You got a press card?" he said, and drank the shot.

I showed him my press card. He examined it like it was a check he didn't want to cash. He handed it back to me. "So, what do you want?"

I told Mazza there were some things about Sandy Pearl's death that bothered me. What I wanted to know from him was what happened the night Sandy Pearl was killed.

"You want the truth—or have you already decided what happened?" He had that defensive-offensive look again, and then he just couldn't hold it back.

"He wasn't drunk!"

I looked at him. "Sandy Pearl wasn't drunk?"

"Absolutely not! The State Liquor Authority wants to lift my license because I got Sandy Pearl drunk and he gets killed. Bullshit! He didn't get drunk here. You know what he had? A spritzer. That's all! A lousy spritzer!"

Being strictly a beer man, I had to ask what a spritzer was.

"Wine and soda. A damned debutante could drink ten of them and still keep her pants on. If she wanted to."

A reporter knows that when he hits somebody who wants to talk—like Hank Mazza did that day—all he has to do is listen. I didn't have to ask anything. Nobody could have shut him up.

The story of Sandy Pearl's death was that he walked out

of Hank Mazza's place at about 11 P.M. on a Wednesday night and staggered out into Mulberry Street into the path of a speeding car. An unidentified man had reached out and tried to pull Sandy back, but it was too late. Neither the driver of the hit-and-run car nor the unidentified man had been found.

"Tell me," I said.

"This guy Pearl was drunk before he got here," Mazza said. "Or else he wasn't drunk at all. He didn't get plastered here. You tell that to the S.L.A. I don't serve falling down drunks."

"Well," I asked, "was he or wasn't he juiced?"

"He didn't look it. I never saw him before. He came in, he wasn't staggering. Who knows? Maybe he's one of these guys who can drink a fifth and still walk straight.

"He comes in. Looks flat-out sober, now. And meets a guy who was already here. They sat back there in the corner. The other guy, now, he had four or five doubles. Red Label Scotch. Not that he's drunk, but he was bending the elbow pretty good."

That was the first I'd heard that somebody was with Sandy that night. "Who was the other guy?"

"I don't know that, either," said Mazza. "It seems to me I've seen him around, you know? But I can't make him."

"Go on."

"Well, they sit in the back for a while. The big guy is drinking doubles, Red Label like I say. Sandy Pearl, he's drinking nothing except a lousy spritzer. I get the feeling they're waiting for somebody else. But whoever it was never showed. After maybe an hour, they leave."

"And Sandy was cold sober?"

Hank Mazza held up both hands, as if to say, "Not so fast."

"Here's the thing," he said, pausing to light another

Benson & Hedges. "Sandy wasn't steady anymore, you get me? He was staggering all over the place."

"You said he wasn't drunk."

"He wasn't. He came in sober, as far as I could see, and he drinks a spritzer. But he staggers out."

"I don't get it."

"That's what happened," Mazza insisted.

"What do you mean? What could have caused it?"

Hank Mazza sipped his Scotch. "There must have been something in that spritzer in addition to wine and soda, see?"

"A knockout drop?" I asked.

Hank Mazza spread out his hands as if to say, "What can I tell you?" He looked at me.

"I told the S.L.A. it wasn't booze," Hank said. "I told them it must have been chloral hydrate. They don't care! Whatever happened, it's my fault."

It squared with what everybody said about Sandy. He wasn't a drinker. He couldn't have been drunk that night.

The rest of Mazza's story was quickly told. Sandy Pearl walked—staggered—out of his place into Mulberry Street, with the other guy right behind him. Once they were out the door, Hank didn't pay much attention.

"I heard a car gun its engine, and then a thump," he said.

"Did you see the guy with Sandy try to pull him back?"

"No. I saw him behind Sandy, but I couldn't see what was happening. It was too dark."

"You say you heard the car gun its engine—and *then* a thump."

"Yeah."

I puffed on my Tiparillo.

"Instead of hitting the brakes, the driver guns the engine?"

Mazza was looking at me like somebody who had just gotten the news that the I.R.S. is going to audit his books. He didn't like the direction my questions were carrying us. I wasn't too pleased with it, myself, but there it was. Somebody wanted to make sure that Sandy would be out on his feet when he walked out of Mazza's.

A macabre comedy routine went through my head: "I've got some good news and some bad news. The good news is that Sandy Pearl wasn't drunk. The bad news is that somebody killed him."

"Listen, Hank, how do you know the guy was trying to pull him back?"

"Well, he was right behind him."

"Maybe he was pushing him."

Hank glared at me. "What?"

"Isn't it possible?"

"Listen, they want my license."

"And I want the guy who murdered Sandy Pearl!" I'd finally said it.

Hank looked at me. "You think that?"

"It's the only thing I can think."

I asked Hank to try to remember anything he could about the other man.

"I didn't pay much attention," said Hank. "He was a fairly big guy—maybe six foot two. Blond guy. Good build. I mean, not sloppy fat or anything. I'd recognize him if I saw him again."

"Did he say anything?"

"I didn't hear much. They were in the back." Hank's eyes flitted and he cocked his head, as though recalling something.

"There was one thing," he said. "I remember the big guy and Sandy were talking as I came up. The big guy says, 'I had a cup of coffee with Pittsburgh.' "

"Who's Pittsburgh?"

Hank shook his head. "I don't know. It just struck me as

21

a funny name, now that I think of it. There can't be too many guys called Pittsburgh."

I walked out onto Mulberry Street and down along the Chinatown playground. There wasn't any indication on the iron fence that a body had been flung against it with deadly force. Now there were several questions chasing themselves around in my head. The $100 bills and the chloral hydrate and the big Red Label Scotch drinker and the car that gunned its engine. Actually, there was a final question—was Sandy being paid off? But I didn't like that question. I put it off.

The time had come for me to talk to the police. I couldn't get the damn business out of my head until I had some answers. I followed the Yellow Brick Road through the plaza to Police Headquarters and presented myself to the homicide bureau.

Lt. Dickson was as lean as a combat recruit fresh out of basic. His hair was iron-gray, and his eyes were like little searchlights. I found out later that he became a lawyer while pounding a beat and now taught law at John Jay College. He was one impressive cop. And he didn't have much time for me.

"Nothing on that case," he said in a voice that made it clear it was closed as far as he was concerned.

You might think that the death of a New York newspaper reporter would send screaming police cars all over the city to round up every possible suspect or near suspect. You might think that murder is a big deal in New York.

Well, it isn't. There's just too much of it for the cops to handle. You have to have a good case to get the attention of the New York City police department. Murder isn't enough. It has to have an angle. The cops are as bad as newspapermen.

Well, anyway, that's why Lt. Dickson wasn't much interested in the case of Sandy Pearl. The police department, first of all, didn't carry it as murder. If they admitted it was murder, they might have to investigate it, if only because Sanford Pearl was a reporter for the *Daily Tribune*.

Lt. Dickson reluctantly let me look at the police report of Sandy's death.

"Listen. This report says Sandy was drunk. How do you know he was?"

Lt. Dickson glared at me. "Do you know how many cases we're stuck with?"

"Sandy Pearl was murdered."

"Listen, Fitzgerald," snapped Dickson. "I'm a busy man. It was a hit-and-run."

"*The Daily Tribune* wants this investigated!" I snapped.

"Oh really?" he smiled. "Have somebody call me."

"Hey, Loot," I said, putting on a friendly face. "I'm not trying to screw up your detail. But Pearl didn't drink. He couldn't have been drunk that night. Will you listen to Hank Mazza?"

"Fitzgerald, do you know how many murders—real murders—outstanding we have right goddam now? Murders that we can't get to?" He held out a sheet of paper and he didn't care whether I wanted to hear about it or not. "Three hundred and eighty-four."

"Goddammit, he didn't drink!"

Lt. Dickson smiled at me. "A newspaper reporter who didn't drink?"

He looked right into me and saw that I was just possibly a trifle smashed from all those Schaefers. The snoopy son of a bitch.

"Excuse me, Fitzgerald. I'm a busy man."

By the time I got home to East 82nd Street that evening, I was still half-buzzing with all those Schaefers and felt a great need to talk this out with someone. I think I even picked up the phone and started to call Chicago before I remembered.

Funny, but the apartment had seemed a hopeful place, a place with a future. Now it seemed uninhabited. Books all over the place. Gibbon's *Decline and Fall of the Roman Empire* sitting on top of Suetonius' *Lives of the Twelve Caesars.* That had surprised Maddy—that a newspaper reporter read ancient Roman history. I remember, too, that I really astounded her by doing a handstand on a bar stool one night at Costello's. Astounded myself as well.

Well, she'd surprised me, too. "I didn't plan it, Fitz. But, see, I got promoted. And there's a guy I used to know. Before you, Fitz. I can't come to New York."

Was that why I'd been dipping into Marcus Aurelius lately? He knew about accepting the unacceptable. The copy of *Meditations* was in my hand.

"Be like the cliff against which the waves continually break; but it stands firm and tames the fury of the water around it."

I might as well, Marcus. Schaefers don't seem to work.

3.

IT came to me with raging suddenness the next morning that Harry Reeves was a loathsome liar. Harry Reeves had declared sneeringly that no self-respecting reporter drank beer. "Sucking on a sissy beer," he had snorted contemptuously. "You can't get drunk on that." Despicable liar.

The valves in my pumpkin yellow Ford Pinto went clickety-clickety-clickety all the way down the FDR Drive, and it sounded on this particular morning like an implacable maniac beating a gong with a sledgehammer inside my right ear.

I parked in the New York Press zone behind police headquarters and lurched to the courthouse. Up the grand stairs to the lobby and to Bennie, the blind news dealer. *Trib*, a *New York Times*, a Pepsi and an Alka-Seltzer. In my stale-aired cubbyhole, before I could even have my Alka-Setzer, there he was, pink-faced and fresh and as maddeningly cheerful as a goddam boiled potato.

"Hot coppers, huh?" he scolded, watching my Pepsi breakfast. "From a few wimpy beers? You know what, Fitzboggen? You're an Orangeman. You're some kind of a left-footed Protestant phony. You're not Irish." I told him what he could do with himself.

"You might want to take a look in Part Five," said Reeves. "Pretty good divorce trial. Mickey Silberman's got this client who used to be a Playboy bunny who's suing a stockbroker. There's going to be oral argument at 11."

"Okay, okay," I muttered, trying to get rid of him.

I thumbed dully through *The Trib*, trying to see past the sun spots dancing in my head. There was an important story there, it occurred to me, but I couldn't get it straight. Finally, I had the Alka-Seltzer, finished the Pepsi, and some of the concrete began to dissolve.

Just before 11, I headed for Part 5 on the third floor, passing over the signs of the zodiac on the floor of the Great Rotunda to the elevators. Part 5, in room 300, is a lofty, wood-paneled place with a New Amsterdam mural on the wall and the venomous splutter of broken marriages in the air.

A dumpy, bald little lawyer was railing at the judge, his voice rising and falling like an orator at a political rally, shaking his fist and calling down the wrath of Justice and Fair Play on one of the greediest and most twisted miscreants in history—the stockbroker. All Mickey Silberman wanted was $1,500 a week temporary alimony for the wilted, distraught one-time Playboy bunny, and counsel fees for himself of a mere $5,000. The stockbroker, than whom no more vile wretch could be imagined, would have to pay.

I slid onto a bench in the front well of the court, next to the judge's bench, where Reeves was already in place.

"Is Silberman what they call in the divorce trade a 'bomber'?" I hissed.

"Listen," snapped Reeves in a loud hush, "wait 'til you hear Weinberg."

I looked across the counsel table before the judge's bench, and there was Bernard W. Weinberg, poised in a sort of eager crouch, waiting impatiently for Silberman to finish.

"They've been kicking each other in the crotch for twenty-five years," said Reeves.

Weinberg didn't wait for his distinguished colleague to finish, but, leaping to his feet like a jack-in-the-box, began flailing away in what soon became a shouting match.

"This woman's spending has reduced my client to penury . . ."

". . . if counsel will show the slightest courtesy . . ."

". . . unable to stand by and accommodate slander . . ."

". . . respect for truth and justice . . ."

". . . hospitalized with anxiety attacks . . ."

". . . once a vibrant beauty . . ."

". . . grasping, greedy . . ."

". . . I did not interrupt respondent's counsel in his flight of imagination . . ."

"Objection, your honor!"

When it was over, we all ended up in the press room downstairs. To me, the new boy in the press room, Mickey smiled. "It's Silberman with a 'b,' not a 'v.' "

"Yeah, listen," Reeves growled to me, "use their names. For Chris' sake, they argued in open court for us."

I crossed the lobby to my own little cubicle press room, and there was Bernard W. Weinberg, patiently waiting.

"A hundred thousand welcomes," he smiled blandly. "Just thought I'd see if you have everything you need."

"I guess so, Counselor," I said.

"If you could use my name, I'd appreciate it," he said. "Lunch?"

So, we all ended up in Giambone's Restaurant behind the Criminal Court Building again, gathered around Reeves's table.

The two old rivals sat across from each other, glaring at each other and flashing fawning smiles at us. Both kept buying drinks for everyone. I could see a hazy pattern developing that would put me in Alcoholics Anonymous within a year. When I tried to pay at least my share of the bill, there was a mad crush of offers from Silberman and Weinberg and so I gave up. But I did discover something while looking into my wallet. One of the $100 bills I'd found in Sandy Pearl's desk was gone.

I'm not ordinarily a suspicious character, but it ran through my mind that I had plunked a bill on the bar at Mazza's Cafe the night before and had gotten nothing like

27

$80 or $90 change. Did I have the bills with me then? I couldn't remember.

It was all still running around in my suspicious little head when I got back to the courthouse and found Schultz the cop waiting for me.

"Hey," he says, "Bennie the news guy's looking for you."

I walked over to the blind news dealer's stand.

"You the *Daily Trib* reporter?"

I pleaded guilty.

"You got a *Trib*, a *Times*, a Pepsi and an Alka-Seltzer?"

"That's right."

"You gave me too much," said Bennie, and held out a $100 bill.

I looked at it. Mazza, forgive me. It was the hangover.

Schultz the cop was standing beside me. "I figured it was you from the way he described you."

Well, it cost me $5 for Blind Bennie and $5 for Schultz and assured that the story would be all over the courthouse.

It also reminded me what that story was in the *Daily Trib* that had caught my eye. There it was on page four—an "artist's sketch" of a guy who had killed a rabbi on an IRT Lexington Avenue subway train.

"Police department sketch by police artist Hugh Wyatt."

It didn't take me long to go down the courthouse steps and follow the Yellow Brick Road between the Manhattan Federal Court Building and the Municipal Building to Police Headquarters to the desk of the standoffish Lt. Dickson of Homicide.

"Fitzgerald, do you think somebody can become a pest on his second visit?" he said. Slam. Bang. The file cabinet drawer shut. He turned and walked into his office. I followed, pushing through the little swinging gate.

"Now, look, Lieutenant," I said, "all I want is for your

28

artist to do a sketch. Like the one of the suspect in the rabbi murder."

"That's a murder case," said Lt. Dickson.

"What can it hurt?"

"What do you want to do with it?"

"Put it in *The Daily Trib*."

"Uh uh! No!"

"Why?"

"Because that makes it a murder case. Because that means I've got to put men on it. Because that means every mistaken do-gooder in all five boroughs will be lighting up my switchboard and filling up my mailbox with phony I.D.s. Because I haven't got the manpower or the patience to put up with any more of this. Goodbye!"

"What the hell would you base the sketch on, anyway?" Lt. Dickson was looking at me with a little less anger.

"Hank Mazza," I said quickly.

"Mazza? What did he see? Some guy who tried to pull him back."

"Or push him."

He was on his feet, walking out of the office, through the little swinging gate, and I trotted behind him. Lt. Dickson did everything on the double, it seemed. "I'm willing to let a sketch be shown around, Fitzgerald. But no publication. You got that?"

You know how many different kinds of noses there are? Not to mention chins. Or foreheads. Hank Mazza sat there, and Hugh Wyatt slid noses at him. Then eyes. Then chins.

Mazza, who didn't seem too comfortable inside Police Headquarters to begin with, lighted a Benson & Hedges.

It took about two hours, but gradually, Wyatt put together a face that Mazza was willing to say looked like the guy who had been with Sandy Pearl that night.

29

"Maybe a little older—maybe a little younger. But that's a lot like him," he said.

"Know him?" said Lt. Dickson.

"Naw."

"He's got a friend named Pittsburgh," I supplied. The piercing eyes turned on me. I was a moth in a candle flame.

"I tell you, I know that face somehow," said Mazza. "I can't quite place it."

I looked at the sketch. A good face, actually. Pretty strong. A wide forehead, good eyes. Clean shaven. Under thirty. "Pittsburgh's pal, who are you?" I thought. "And why did you push Sandy in front of that car?"

Lt. Dickson had called me an instant pest, and I guess that's what I became. Everywhere I went, I shoved that sketch of Pittsburgh's friend into everybody's face. At Giambone's, several guys lingered tantalizingly over it. Like Hank Mazza, they could almost make the guy, but not quite. The sketch wasn't quite right? The guy had changed his looks some?

"What's the matter with you?" Harry Reeves looked at me as though I were some kind of mutant. "Goddam Boy Scout! Will you stop pestering people with that stupid sketch?"

"Harry, you old fossil, I'm telling you this guy shoved Sandy in front of that car."

Harry studied me a few moments. "Schultz the cop says you walk around with $100 bills."

I guess I froze a bit.

"Oh. Yeah. I gave it to Blind Bennie by mistake."

"Listen, Fitzboggen, it's none of my business, see?" said Reeves. "I wouldn't leave money like that lying around."

When I got to the courthouse the next day, the *Women's Wear Daily* reporter who shared my little cubicle told me a girl had called.

"Who was it?"

"I don't know, but she sounded pretty sexy," said Miltie. He rolled his eyes around like Groucho Marx. So Maddy was having second thoughts about coming to New York? My spirits began to rise as hope swelled back through me.

"You wouldn't happen to recognize this guy?" I said, offering the sketch to Miltie.

"Who is it?"

"Nobody," I said. "A Boy Scout."

I tossed the sketch into a drawer, slammed it shut, and wondered if I should go ahead and spend those $100 bills. By the end of that day, I had almost forgotten the whole thing. Then the phone rang, and it was a woman.

"Sandy?"

"Hello? Who do you want?"

"Sandy Pearl."

My heart began going a little faster. "Who is this?"

"What?"

"Are you a personal friend of Sandy's?"

"Yes. Is Sandy there?"

"Say, who is this?"

"Just a friend."

"Now, listen, Miss, I'm a friend of Sandy's, too. I guess you haven't heard. Listen, Sandy's dead."

There was a stifled gasp.

"Hello?"

"Oh, my god—no!"

"I'm sorry. But, look, maybe you can help me. I'm trying to find out how it happened. I've got a sketch I'd like you to look at . . ."

She wasn't on the line any more.

4.

I'LL say this for Harry Reeves. He never asked me about that $100 bill again. I was so curious about why he wasn't curious that I almost asked him why he didn't ask me about it. The bills snuggled in my wallet, and every time I noticed them I thought about Sandy Pearl again. And that would spur me to show the sketch of Pittsburgh's friend around. I might as well have shown it to Blind Bennie for all the good it did.

She was slim and dark with dusky gray eyes and she strolled into my cubbyhole office asking for directions to the county clerk's office.

"Jury notice," she said. "Where do I go?"

I was about to say, "To lunch with me." But I restrained myself and directed her back through the rotunda to the jury qualification room.

I sat through a boring hearing about the City of New York's financial plight and heard the City Corporation Counsel wail that there was no way the city could pay back $1.6 billion in outstanding bonds. I was back in the office trying to figure out a way to write the thing so it wouldn't put everybody to sleep, when Miltie the *Women's Wear Daily* reporter walked in.

"One of those Playboy bunny divorcées was here looking for you," he said, doing his Groucho Marx eyebrow elevation.

"Yeah? Who was she?"

"I don't know, but she looked like Elizabeth Ashley."

I went back to the boring bonds story because that didn't register. People have the idea that these complex financial

32

stories are so difficult to do because you need deep economic expertise. Totally irrelevant. They're just like any other story, except that nobody's interested in them but people who own stocks and bonds. That reduces the number of readers to some insignificant fraction.

Out of my left eye, I suddenly realized the Mediterranean Vision was standing in the doorway watching me quizzically. I looked up to make sure. It was she, all right—the dusky beauty with the jury notice. I glanced at Miltie, and he was grinning like an idiot. He nodded his head to indicate that she was the Playboy bunny he was talking about. She walked across to my typewriter, and I suddenly understood that poem about the silky lady whose sinuous movements inspired the line, "How sweetly flows the liquefaction of her clothes."

"Find the jury qualification room all right?" I asked.

"Oh, yes," she said, and took out a cigarette. "Thanks." She stood there holding the cigarette. The municipal bonds story became not only boring but positively intrusive. I lighted her cigarette for her.

She asked me where to catch the Independent subway, and gabbed about what a drag it was to have to spend two weeks sitting on a jury.

"It must be fascinating to be a reporter," she smiled.

Well. I don't need a house to fall on me.

"I'm Ed Fitzgerald. *Daily Tribune*."

"Rita," she said. "Rita Meoli."

That annoying multimillion-dollar municipal bond story flew out of my Texas Instruments Silent 700 portable typewriter in ten minutes after that, and I phoned it in to the wire room. We walked across Foley Square, up past the monolithic Fort Zinderneuf black marble Family Court Building to Doyle's Pub.

"Schaefer," I said. "White wine," she said. She had a

33

Pall Mall in her slender fingers; I had a Tiparillo between my teeth. I put the world on hold.

"You know how it is when you put the world on hold?" I asked her. "You just put everything down where it is and say, 'I'll be back later'? Well, that's what I'm doing right now, Rio Rita."

She laughed in that wonderfully inviting way; raven hair and fetching figure—the treacherous Madilyn Healy of Chicago no longer existed.

"Me, too," she said.

"So, what do you do when you're not on jury duty?"

"Not much. I've always wanted to be in your business."

"The newspaper business?"

"I used to think I could write. Mostly poetry though."

"You have any place you have to go?" I asked her cautiously.

"No."

"Nobody waiting for you?"

She gave me that smile again. "I'm divorced. I've got nothing waiting for me except an empty apartment. Going home to that doesn't interest me at the moment."

Going home to that suddenly began to interest me very much.

"Do you have to be a lawyer to write about the court?"

"Naw," I told her. "People think that. Hell, Sandy Pearl couldn't hardly read *Peanuts,* but he was a damn good court reporter."

"Who's Sandy Pearl?"

"Ah, well, this little guy I replaced."

"He retired?"

"Yeah. Permanently."

She looked puzzled.

"Dead."

"Oh," she said. "What happened?"

"Well, Rita, I'll tell you what happened. Somebody knocked him off, see?"

Did you ever see blood drain from somebody's face? You've read that phrase, but did you ever see it happen? Somebody's reasonably pinky-brown flesh colored and all of a sudden they go white like a piece of chalk. That's what happened to Rita when I told her Sandy had been knocked off.

"Murdered?" she said in a little gasp.

"You got it."

"How? I never read anything about any reporter getting murdered."

"Well, dammit, Rita, the cops don't call it murder. Nobody calls it murder—except me. But it was, it was!"

Well, the color came back to that lovely face.

"Oh."

"What do you mean, 'Oh'?"

She even smiled a little. "Some reporters sometimes get a little carried away maybe?"

"Rita, did you call me up about Sandy once?"

"What?" She seemed genuinely puzzled.

"It was you, wasn't it?"

She reached over and took my hand and squeezed it. "Oh, Eddie—no. Of course not. I don't know any Sandy."

I believed her. I had the damned case on the brain. The world was on hold, but somehow it kept getting signals through to me.

"I'm just a girl who's finally come to terms with the fact that she's divorced and alone," Rita said. "I'd probably talk to you about anything to keep from going home to that empty apartment." Black hair and gray eyes and a laugh deep in her throat that went through me made me believe anything she said. I didn't want to go home to an empty apartment, either. If she found me attractive and entertaining, I found her fascinating and a little wistful.

We had fettucini Alfredo at Forlini's at the edge of Chinatown behind the Tombs, and then I took her to East 82nd Street. Ah, dear world, is there anything so unreservedly delicious as the newly revealed charms of a beautiful brunette?

"It's been so long," she moaned once, which was surely a terrible waste of one of our greatest natural resources. We went from life to death and back again over and over in a sexual frenzy, and the only flaw in a glorious love bout was once when she murmured a name and it wasn't mine. "Tony," she whimpered. Well, under the circumstances, I decided to overlook it.

Afterwards, we lay in bed smoking for a while, and she snuggled up under my arm as though trying to graft herself onto me. We dozed and wakened, and loved again. It would have been a perfect evening except for that "Tony."

"I have to go," she finally said.

"Go?"

"I'm sorry."

I looked at the clock. It was two in the morning.

Well, what the hell, I got up and we got dressed and left. When we got outside, she kissed me and said, "You don't have to drive me home, Eddie. I'll get a cab."

No way I'd let her take a cab, but she insisted. "It's way out in Brooklyn," she said. She walked off toward Second Avenue, and I had to follow. I couldn't talk her out of it—nothing would do but a cab. Well, I hailed one and put her inside and kissed her again.

"I'll call you," I said through the window, and then the cab was bouncing down Second Avenue catching up with the lights.

I stood there a moment dreaming of future Mediterranean cruises, and didn't see the hurtling shape until it was almost too late. I heard and sensed it more than saw it, actually. The gunned engine, the onrushing mass leaping over the rumpled avenue. I dived over the hood of a parked Volkswagen, and the side of the racing car grazed my right shoe. Then it was gone, speeding south down Second Avenue, blending in with the traffic and other taillights, and I was sprawled on the sidewalk breathing hard and terrified out of my mind.

5.

I don't know how long I lay there on the sidewalk, breathing hard; I guess until I saw the car disappear. It wouldn't take a genius to figure out that I'd stirred up something this time. Somebody had walked into my press office and had seen that sketch on the wall, or had heard me asking around about the man who was with Sandy Pearl in Mazza's Cafe, or had heard about the $100 bills. Whoever had killed Sandy Pearl was after me. My god, I'd shown that sketch to just about everybody I'd met around Foley Square. A cast of thousands. At least, though, I finally knew for certain that there was something behind all this. And it had to be something pretty big. I also realized I had a tiger by the tail, and that I had to unravel the story of who killed Sandy before I became a part of that story. I had heard angels' wings beating when that car almost clipped me.

Dr. Johnson once observed that it concentrates a man's mind wonderfully if he knows he's going to be hanged, and I agree with that now. All I could think of was Sandy and the $100 bills and the face of the man who was a friend of Pittsburgh's. And what about Rita? Had she set me up? Or had somebody followed us? The moment I got inside my joint, I started to check on Rita. For god's sake—I didn't even have her address! The telephone number she had given me, I now figured, would be no good. I called it. I was right. I tried information for all five boroughs of New York—no Rita Meoli.

I arrived at Foley Square the next morning hung over, bleary eyed, exhausted and jumpy as a bullfrog. Alka-Seltzer, Pepsi Cola, hurry across the lobby to Harry Reeves's press room to get some answers.

Reeves shook his head and looked me over. "Huh! You went out last night and mixed with a bunch of Orangemen and now you come in here looking like a three-day-old cow chip."

"Harry . . ."

"You go out with a slather of left-footers and suck on a sissy beer and when the tab comes nobody wants to pay it. Then they throw you down the stairs."

"Listen, Harry," I said. "Something happened last night. This beautiful broad came into my office and put the make on me."

Well, that was the wrong thing to say to Harry.

"Put the make on you?" he snorted. "An Orangeman with all the sex appeal of a skid row wino?"

I was a fool on a fool's errand, of course, but I checked with the jury qualification clerk to see if, just by chance, Rita Meoli had been in to report for jury duty. No luck. I hurried around to the county clerk's office to see if her name was even on the list of the prospective jurors in Manhattan. No Rita Meoli. I still didn't know whether Rita had set me up to get killed or whether I had been followed.

I wish I could tell you that I did not go to lunch at Giambone's that day with Reeves and Judge Nacht the Magician.

Clams on the half-shell came, and tortellini and pasta and Soave Bolla and osso bucco and bombs and Schaefer and B. & B. and Grand Marnier. Magic acts came and tall tales of courtroom derring-do and snips of political skullduggery memorable for their dire results. You could get spoiled at Giambone's.

Eventually, they all drifted away and I was left with Reeves. There was nothing much doing at the courthouse that afternoon, so we sat over yet another drink.

"Now, listen, motor mouth—don't explode. Did Sandy Pearl get in on these lunches?"

Harry looked grumpy. "Aw, Jesus! No, I told you. There was always the chance he'd have to pick up a tab!"

I had to find a nice way to word it. "If you didn't want to come to lunch, would these lawyers—try to slip you something?"

"What's the matter with you? Somebody buys you lunch and you start that?"

So much for my diplomacy.

"All I'm wondering . . ."

"You're wondering if Sandy Pearl was on the take? Who the hell knows? Could he be? Sure he could. Any reporter who wants to could be. You can get paid for every time you mention a lawyer's name, if you want. It's been done."

"Yeah? How much?"

Reeves shook his head. "How much?" He looked at me. "If you mean could he get a hundred bucks—sure."

I'd really fooled old Harry, all right.

"Not necessarily . . ."

"What the hell are you up to?"

"Goddammit, Harry, I'm telling you there's something fishy. He's got fishhooks in his pocket, right? He's got no money, right? Well, maybe somebody was paying him off. He had money."

Harry smiled that knowing look of a man with an ace in the hole. "Sure he had money. From his wife."

"His wife?"

"Marcia is her name. Independently wealthy. And she made a couple of commercials about, I don't know, toilet paper, and made a bundle more. Now, will you for Chris' sake get off it?"

All that pasta and Soave Bolla and Reeves talking sense to me made me wonder if that car really had tried to blow me away.

When I got back to my little office, there was a message to

call Al Wagner. I ran over to the other press room and asked Harry who Al Wagner was.

"Al Wagner? Surrogate's Court."

Surrogate's Court? That's where wills and estates and guardianships of various kinds are handled, and it's in a different building, across the street and down at the foot of Foley Square. As a general rule, we tried to avoid going over there because we don't want our city desks to consider us responsible for that beat.

I walked back to my office and called Al Wagner.

"Who?" he said. "Ted? Ted who?" I kept telling him it was Ed but I don't think he ever got it straight.

"Well, Mr. Pearl told me to remind him about the Amster Case," he said.

"Amster Case?"

"It's on for the twelfth."

"What's the Amster Case?"

"Well, you'll have to come over and dig it out, Ted," he replied plaintively. "I got no time to go through those papers. Mr. Pearl said to remind him."

That's all I could get out of Wagner, the clerk from the Manhattan Surrogate's Court. I was already "watching" about a dozen other cases that court clerks, lawyers, judges and plaintiffs had called me about. When I mentioned it to Reeves he said the name didn't ring a bell with him, so I put it aside, figuring to take a look on the twelfth—if I had the time.

Then I beat it down the long steps and over past St. Andrews through the Yellow Brick Road to Police Headquarters. When I tried to tell Lt. Dickson about my scrape with immortality, he seemed loftily disinterested. How had I done with the sketch?

"Well, it obviously worked."

He turned his lamps on me.

"Somebody got excited enough about that sketch to try to run me over," I explained.

Well, Lt. Dickson would not work up a sketch of Rita Meoli. He did check the record, just to make sure, and found nothing on her.

I was unable to describe the car that tried to cream me, or the driver, or any other damn thing. Not only isn't murder enough, attempted murder isn't either. I left.

After that, Sandy Pearl began once more to recede in my mind. More pressing problems engulfed me as the courthouse and its myriad calendars, motions and trials overwhelmed me. I might have forgotten it altogether, except that one day I was up in the *Daily Trib* main office to check some clippings about an approaching judicial election. I was walking toward the newspaper clipping library, passing the sports department, when Sam Papa, the baseball writer, said something that stuck in my head.

"I remember Juffras," said Sam. "He had a cup of coffee with Cincinnati."

That stopped me. I went into sports.

"Hey, Sam!"

"Well, well," he grinned, "if it isn't Lamont Cranston."

"Who?"

"Fitz, since you went to the Supreme Court, nobody knows where the hell you are. You're the Shadow!"

"Thanks a lot," I said. "What was that about somebody having a cup of coffee with Cincinnati?"

"Bob Juffras. Couldn't go to his right."

"But what about the other guy?"

"What other guy?"

"Cincinnati."

Sam looked at me. "Cincinnati is the Reds. They're a major league baseball team. They have been known to win pennants. They have been known to bury a team called the Yankees. Wake up, Fitz!"

It took a certain amount of this kind of flak, but finally Sam explained it to me. "Look, Fitz, when a guy gets a tryout with a Major League team but doesn't stick, they say he had a cup of coffee with that team."

"Pittsburgh!" I said. "The guy had a tryout with the Pittsburgh Pirates!"

"Not Pittsburgh. Cincinnati."

That was it. My sketch—my face—must have been a ballplayer once.

"Listen, Sam, you think you'd recognize a ballplayer who once had a tryout with the Pirates?"

"Who is he?"

"I don't know, Sam. But I've got to find out."

I went clickety-clickety down the FDR Drive in my yellow pumpkin, ran into the courthouse and grabbed the police sketch by Hugh Wyatt, and dashed back to the car. When I got back to the *Trib* and ran the sketch into the sports department, Sam Papa looked it over carefully.

"Naw, I can't place him, Fitz."

"Look, Sam, you've got to. Look closely."

There was the open, ingenuous face, the clear, steady eyes. He looked like a ballplayer, now that I knew that about him. I shaded the top of the face to make it look like he was wearing a baseball cap.

"Nope."

"Who would know, Sam? I've got to find out."

"Maybe somebody at the *Sporting News*."

I beat it over to the *Sporting News*, the so-called Bible of Baseball, and was shown to the desk of an ancient gentleman wearing a vest and thick glasses. After my problem was explained, I took out the police sketch and carefully, hopefully, laid it before him.

The old gentleman took one look and nodded his head.

"Arny Hayes," he said. "Outfield."

"You're sure?"

The old gentleman looked at me in surprise. "Yes, young man, I'm sure. I've been covering minor league baseball for forty years. Arny Hayes was a fine prospect. Could run like Joe Morgan. Arm like Joe Rudi. Led the International League in hitting one year."

"What happened to him?"

"Well, now, as I recall he got in trouble with the law. I've got something on it, I think."

He got up and walked ramrod straight to a filing cabinet marked "Pirates." From an envelope he dug out a clipping, and there was a photograph of a younger Arny Hayes looking out, wearing the uniform of the Pirates, with palm trees in the background. The clipping was one of those colorful sports stories asking whether Arny Hayes "could fill the legendary spikes of Roberto Clemente."

"Here it is," my baseball historian said. "Yes. Trouble with the law."

"What kind of case?" I asked.

He looked at the clipping. "Well, it looks from this story like he killed somebody."

6.

IT was one of those routine tragedies that glare out at you from the newspapers every day. Arny Hayes, hopeful Major League outfielder, goes to spring training with the Pirates and has his cup of coffee. Not this year, Arny, is the verdict, and Arny goes back home to Milford, New Jersey. Soon, he'll be spending another year in the International League. Arny goes into New York City for a drink. He has quite a few drinks. Then he has some more. Finally he settles down to serious drinking. By that time, a skinny redhead from Staten Island is with him. Arny tells Marjorie Keller, a secretary who works at the World Trade Center, about how he once hit a grand-slam homer to beat the Birmingham Barons. "That's really something," says Marjorie.

"Another boilermaker here," says Arny to the bartender at the Pirate's Cove on the West Side.

"I didn't know ballplayers were allowed to drink," says Marjorie.

For some reason, Arny Hayes laughs loud and long.

At the end of that night, when it was almost five o'clock in the morning, Arny started driving Marjorie Keller home to Staten Island, going down the West Side Highway and heading toward the Brooklyn-Battery Tunnel that would lead through Brooklyn to the Verrazano Narrows Bridge. Arny Hayes handled his Mustang with easy, athletic grace, zipping along between the iron uprights under the roadway beside the Hudson River in lower Manhattan. He saw the Volkswagen stalled in the roadway at the last second, and swerved at high speed into an iron girder. And Marjorie Keller was dead.

Arny was in Beekman Downtown Hospital for six weeks.

His left ankle had been shattered, broken in a dozen places. On the fifth day, he learned about Marjorie Keller from an assistant Manhattan district attorney who informed Arny that he had been indicted by a grand jury on charges of drunken driving and vehicular homicide. Arny limped out of the hospital on a crutch, with his left foot in a cast, and went to the Ericcson Place Police Station to be booked, and then to the Manhattan Criminal Court Building to be arraigned.

I read all this in the *Daily Trib* clips. The lawyer who had defended him was Bernard Weinberg, my pasty-faced little friend who spoke Gaelic. And Weinberg had gotten Arny off with a plea-bargained reduction from vehicular homicide to "driving while impaired." Three years probation.

Lt. Dickson looked at me with elaborate annoyance. "What do you mean, pick him up?"

"But, Loot, that's the guy."

"Are you ready to sign an affidavit that this guy pushed Sandy Pearl in front of that car?"

"Mazza will!"

"Wanna bet?"

"So can't you bring him in for questioning?"

"He lives in Jersey."

"So what are you going to do about it?"

"Nothing."

The woman's voice sounded very friendly and middle-class over the phone from Milford, New Jersey, until I mentioned her son.

"Oh, I'm sorry. Arny isn't here."

Did she know where her son was?

"He lives in the city somewhere. I haven't heard from him lately."

So, there you were. Another walking wounded had disappeared somewhere into the Big Apple. I checked with Bernie Weinberg.

"Arny Hayes?" he said with seeming uncertainty. "Let me see." We stood in the great rotunda of the courthouse, under the circle of murals depicting the law from Hammurabi to Thomas Jefferson. "The boy who killed that secretary in the auto crash?" He smiled at his feat of memory.

"You know where I can find him?"

Weinberg shook his head. "Maybe I have an address in the office."

But later on when I checked with him, Weinberg said he had no current address. "Did you try his mother in Milford, New Jersey?"

I kept coming up with blanks. Rita Meoli. Arny Hayes. Where were they?

I came off the Verrazano Narrows Bridge onto Staten Island and headed south down Hylan Boulevard, down past all the new houses that have gone up willy-nilly in the boom that followed the opening of the bridge. And I was in New Dorp. The house was white frame, and not much to look at. A little yard in front with some grass trying to grow.

The lady who answered my knock was faded and washed-out, as though all of the vitality had long since abandoned her body. She looked at me with little interest.

"I'm sorry to bother you, Mrs. Keller. I'm Ed Fitzgerald, the reporter who called."

She started to close the door. "I told you I'm not interested in talking about it," she said. But it wasn't as easy as hanging up on me, as she had done earlier.

"Please, Mrs. Keller."

There was no real fight in her. She shrugged and let me in.

"He tried to give me money, that boy who killed my Margie," she said. "But I wouldn't let him buy a clear con-

47

science with money. He can rot in hell." A spark of fire was there yet, smoldering beneath that dead shell.

"Can you tell me where to find him, Mrs. Keller?"

"He wrote me. I think I have a letter someplace. What do you want with him?"

"Well, it's complicated."

She opened a secretary and pulled out a little drawer. In it, she found a letter and handed it to me. "That's it," she said. "If you talk to that boy who killed my Margie, tell him I hope he rots in hell."

I didn't know what to say. The years of emptiness that come afterward aren't ever in those casual horror stories on the front page.

Arny Hayes's address was way out in Queens, out in Far Rockaway on the Atlantic Ocean. It took nearly two hours to drive out there, through Brooklyn and over the Marine Parkway Bridge and out along Rockaway.

It was one of those beachfront wooden frames off Seagirt Boulevard, and it seemed to me a lot like Mrs. Keller's little white bungalow in New Dorp. Arny hadn't salvaged much from his dreams, either, it appeared. There was a wind-swept porch in front, and a bleak look to the place. I knocked and rang the bell. No sign of anybody there.

I walked around the back and peeked in through the back door. I couldn't see much, and I was about to leave when the back door gave under my weight. It swung open slowly, and then I saw that the door jamb was splintered. Even then I was about to get out of there, but I saw an Adidas striped sneaker protruding from behind the kitchen wall. I stepped in.

"Arny?"

I pushed the door all the way open and walked into the kitchen. The Adidas sneaker didn't stir. I walked over and looked around the wall into the hallway. Arny Hayes lay there, face down, and the hair on the back of his head was bathed in blood. I didn't have to look any closer. There was about him that rigid total stillness that means a dead body.

Panic sprang up in me. I looked around, shaky and trembling. But there was no sound. Nothing. I saw the phone and started toward it when I noticed the wire had been cut. I beat it out of there as fast as I could without touching anything.

Ironhead Matthews was admirably calm, under the circumstances. He promised to have Tony Casale from the Queens shack out to take a photograph within 15 minutes. Then I could call the police.

"Well, Jesus, Ironhead, he's lying there stiff as a board!"

"Casale's on the way. As soon as he gets there, call the cops."

"Okay."

"What the hell's it all about, anyway, Fitz?"

So, Casale got out there in a radio car and I put in a call to Lt. Dickson.

"He's what—dead?"

"Loot, I finally tracked him down out in Far Rockaway, and when I got there he was stretched out on the floor—shot in the head."

"You're sure he's dead?"

"I'm no coroner, Loot, but he's not moving."

"Goddammit!"

Casale got his pictures just as the squad cars started rolling up. In about 20 minutes, the place was surrounded. And after a while, even Lt. Dickson showed up, scowling and muttering.

"Well, you dug something up this time, didn't you?"

He acted as though I'd done it on purpose.

"For Chris' sake, Loot, *I* didn't shoot him."

Well, you might have seen Casale's photograph of Arny Hayes's Adidas sneaker sticking out of the hall. It was on the front page the next morning, along with my story. There was nothing in it about Sandy Pearl. It was carried as the "mystery slaying" of a one-time ballplayer. It was that, all right. The whole damn thing came down on my head. Nobody had been interested before, but now the shit hit the fan. Somehow, since I'd caused the murder and the mess, I was supposed to have the answers.

7.

I had wanted a detective on the Pearl case. Well, now I had two—Dan Langner and Marty Stevens. That's the way it is with cops. They only come in pairs. They were waiting for me when I walked into my cubbyhole press room. Big Dan Langner had once been a basketball star at Archbishop Malloy High School, and his partner Marty Stevens was a smooth-looking guy who resembled a TV game show emcee. Langner had Arny Hayes's criminal file with him, and he went over it from beginning to end, trying to find possible suspects.

"What about Mrs. Keller?" he said.

"Who?"

"The mother of the girl Arny killed in that car crash."

The faded image of that ruined lady leaped into my head, and I shook my head. "No way."

Dan Langner went on, "This Marjorie Keller. No boy friend. Her father was dead. Nobody but her mother. Couldn't the mother have shot this guy?"

"She's got an ironclad alibi," I said. "She was with somebody when the M.E. figures Arny was shot."

"Yeah? Who?" said Langner.

"Me."

"That's right. You were there that same day."

Stevens opened the criminal file. "Okay, the deceased plea-bargained out on this matter. The lawyer was Bernard Weinberg."

"Did you talk to him?" I asked.

"Yeah. Doesn't know a thing."

From what anybody knew, there seemed to be no reason why anyone would want to kill Arny Hayes. The investiga-

51

tion showed that he had seemingly lost all interest in life after the Marjorie Keller death. He had continued to drink heavily, had drifted into Greenwich Village, and finally had rented a bungalow out in Far Rockaway. He had wandered along the beaches, doing very little, shriveled by what had happened to him.

"Was he into loan sharks?" asked Langner.

"I don't know," I said.

"Did he play the horses? Was it another woman?"

"You got me," I said.

"What did he have to do with Sandy Pearl?"

"That, my friend, is the question."

"Anything you haven't mentioned?" said Langner. I jerked slightly, I'm afraid, but he didn't seem to notice.

"I'll tell you the truth, Langner, I don't know. I've gone over all this so many times, I don't know what I've told you and Dickson and what I haven't. It's all a big blur."

Stevens closed the file. They stood up together.

"We'll be in touch," said Langner.

Not long afterward in walked Bernard Weinberg, all smiles and charm.

"Well, my busy friend," he said. "I see you're already in the papers. Your friends the police came to see me."

"It wasn't my idea," I said lamely.

"No, no, no, they should have." He smiled his parchment-paper smile. "I told them everything I knew. A tragic case. I'm only happy I was able to save that boy some anguish at one time."

"I don't suppose you've got any idea why anybody would want to kill him?"

Weinberg shook his head sadly. "One can only imagine. A case like that. The city's full of savage people. You never know."

"Do you know if Arny knew Sandy Pearl?"

Weinberg rocked back on his heels and pondered the ceiling. "Sandy Pearl—ah, yes—your predecessor here. No, no, I don't know. Seems unlikely, though. I doubt that Arny was ever in this building. It all happened in the Criminal Court Building."

John the information booth clerk tapped on the glass as I went by. John's usual routine was to come in and go over the racing charts for the day. Then he'd go over to the Off-Track Betting office on Broadway and get down his bets. He'd stop at Brady's for a couple of belts, and then stroll back to the courthouse. The most asked question at John's information booth was, "Hey, where's the guy who's supposed to be in the information booth?" But even John knew all about the Arny Hayes case.

"Hey! This the guy whose drawing you were showing around?" He waved the *Daily Trib* at me. "So you found him, huh?"

You could say that.

"Yeah, John. Now, all I need to know is what he had to do with Sandy Pearl."

John cupped a hand behind his bad right ear. "Sandy? Oh, the little fellah who was here before you? What'd he do?"

I explained as best I could that I thought somebody knocked him off.

"Huh!" said John. "Quiet little guy. Hardly said a word to anybody. Girl from the office used to bring him his pay, and sometimes he'd put a deuce on a horse with me."

I went back into my press room and was shuffling the messages when it finally penetrated. I took one of the plain white envelopes out of the desk drawer and went back out to the information booth.

"What girl used to bring Sandy his pay, John?"

"What?" he said, cupping his hand behind his tin right ear.

"Who brought his pay?"

"Well, she was a good looker, see. I thought maybe it was his wife, ya know? But then I saw his wife on a TV commercial once, and it wasn't her. She used to bring him his pay."

I took out an envelope and showed it to him. "In a white envelope like this?"

"Yeah, yeah," said John. "That's it."

"She was good looking, did you say?"

"Yeah. Nice, you know?"

"Was she brunette?"

"Right. Dark hair. Stylish dresser."

The pleasing vision of Rita Meoli swam up in my mind. I kept grilling poor deaf old John unmercifully, but that was all he could tell me—only that from his vantage point in the huge, vaulted lobby, he could watch everybody come and go, and that he had seen the beautiful, stylish brunette bring envelopes to Sandy every so often.

I sat at my desk chomping on a Tiparillo. Sandy was blackmailing some attractive brunette for $100 a throw for something? Rita Meoli? She was paying him for stud services?

As I came out and started through the lobby, I saw her looking quizzically at the list of courthouse offices. She glanced at me—a trim, aristocratic blonde with nervous blue eyes—and then she smiled.

"Could you direct me to the county clerk's office?"

She wasn't as strikingly beautiful as Rita Meoli, but she was a handsome woman with an appealing, even inviting face. She seemed hesitant, unsure of herself, as though spying on reporters was not her ordinary occupation.

"Straight ahead to the rotunda, and then to the right," I told her.

"Thank you," she said, and walked away, swaying on her heels in a graceful walk not calculated to entice. I lighted my Tiparillo and waited. She would have to walk to the rotunda and make a show of going into the clerk's office before she could come back and pick me up.

I heard her heels clicking on the granite floor soon afterward, and she came walking back out. As she passed, I smiled.

"Why don't we have a drink?"

She darted a look at me that was a mixture of fright and astonishment, showing both vulnerability and annoyance. She kept walking and said nothing.

I was beginning to hallucinate.

8.

THE next morning I was digging through the desk drawer for some court papers when I found that yellow legal pad Sandy had left. There was that triple underlined number—2381. It taunted me. When I had first seen that number, I didn't realize what it was, but now I decided it had to be an index number. That's how you track down court cases. The only trouble was it wasn't all there. Sandy had jotted down 2381. But you have to have the year in which it had been filed for it to be of any use. In other words, an index number of 2381/82 would mean that the case was the 2,381st case filed in 1982. I went down to the county clerk's room in the basement and got Billy the assistant clerk to steer me. Case 2381/82 was listed as "Terry Windsor versus Gruchala Publishing Co.," which publishes *Flash Magazine*.

A quick scan of the court papers revealed that Terry was a model of unblemished and virginal reputation who was shocked, amazed and distressed because somehow a wicked photographer had taken photographs of her in the nude and had brazenly published them in *Flash Magazine* without her knowledge or consent. The photographs had caused her shame, humiliation and scalding embarrassment and she would feel a lot better if she could collect $100,000 in damages. Sandy Pearl was following some interesting cases. Number 2381 for 1981 was a negligence case, and the same number for 1980 was an election fraud. The two years before that were cases about a dress business and somebody suing New York City for a broken foot caused by stepping into a pothole in front of City Hall. As far as I could see, they were all dead ends. I rode the elevator back up to the main floor thinking that maybe Reeves was right and that I should forget the whole thing. I was getting dizzy from all the loose ends.

That afternoon, in walked Dan Langner and Marty Stevens, looking poker-faced but pretty jaunty. They both sat down, and Dan took out a little notebook.

"Well, Fitzgerald," he said, "it's all wrapped up."

I looked at him in considerable surprise. "You know who killed Arny?"

"Yep," he said. Marty Stevens nodded.

"Who?"

"Well, let me lay it out for you," said Langner. He flipped a page in his notebook. "The deceased was heavily in debt. The landlord said he was about to get bounced from that bungalow. He had run up tabs at every bar and grocery store along Far Rockaway."

"He owed everybody," said Marty Stevens.

"This girl who lived down the street? Janet Ijams? She was kind of sweet on him, it turns out. She says he needed a lot of money and didn't know how to get it."

"He needed money?" I asked. "What for?"

"Loan sharks."

Marty Stevens nodded. "The shysters were into him, Fitzgerald."

"The loan sharks killed him?"

Dan Langner closed his notebook. "That's it."

How do you like that? I shook my head. "Who were they?"

"Could have been guys out of Sheepshead Bay. Coney Island."

I looked at Langner and then at Stevens. "You mean you don't know who the loan sharks are?"

No, they didn't know. It wasn't the kind of homicide that ever got solved. It was enough that they knew what had happened to Arny. It was a familiar story. A guy down on his luck went to the loan sharks and the day came when he had to pay and couldn't.

"It doesn't have anything to do with Sandy Pearl's murder at all?"

Dan Langner smiled. "We have no reason to consider Sandy Pearl's death to be homicide, don't forget."

So that was it. All tied up nice and neat, and case closed. Back to square one.

"You need anything more for your story?" said Langner.

"Story?"

"Wrapping the case up."

"Without an arrest? No indictment—nothing?"

"Fitzgerald, I just explained that to you."

"Another death by persons unknown?"

They looked at each other. Langner put his notebook into an inside pocket of his jacket. They got up and walked out. I called Lt. Dickson and was told the Arny Hayes case was now dormant. Closed? Not closed. But nothing more would be done until or unless other developments surfaced.

Well, I didn't write a glowing, complimentary story about how big shot Langner and his smoothie pal Marty Stevens had cleared up the murder of the mysterious ballplayer. I wasn't putting their names in the paper with that piece of fiction.

Two days later, the story leaped out of *The Daily Tribune* at me. All about how two veteran Manhattan South Homicide detectives had cleared up the mystery slaying of Arny Hayes. It was by Dubbs Brewer. I grabbed the phone.

"Hey, Dubbs—what's this Hayes story?"

"Pretty nice, huh?"

"Dubbs, for Chris' sake, they're blowing smoke up your

58

ass! They solved nothing! Goddammit, what about Sandy Pearl?"

"What about him?"

"Aw, Jesus, Dubbs—forget it."

I walked around in a stupor that day, muttering to myself about the stupidity of cops in general and Dan Langner in particular. They had lied and Dubbs had sworn to it. When I tried to complain to Ironhead Matthews, he wanted to know why I was spending all that time on Sandy Pearl anyway.

"That's not your beat."

I was too tired to quarrel with him.

I wasn't prepared for the call. I had the phone in my hand and wasn't really listening at first. The woman was weepy and rambling and mad as hell. "My Arny didn't gamble!" she raged. "That's a lie! You said in your story my Arny went to loan sharks. If he did, he wanted money for that woman—the mother of that woman."

It was Mrs. Hayes railing at me. Even though I hadn't written the story, I'm the one who had called her up.

A figure swam up in the doorway. Standing there, smiling, was attorney-at-law Michael Silberman.

"Care for a drink?"

I had written a story about one of Silberman's signal victories the day before. I'd already forgotten about it.

"Rain check, Silberman."

He nodded and left.

I sat there, having a last Tiparillo before heading uptown. The phone rang.

"Fitzgerald, *Daily Tribune*, here."

The voice was hesitant. "Mr. Fitzgerald?"

"Yes."

"I talked to you before. You're Sandy's friend."

I tried not to tense up. "You called before?"

"I'm sorry I hung up on you, Mr. Fitzgerald. When you told me about Sandy . . ."

It wasn't Rita Meoli. It was the other girl who had called, the one who had panicked when I told her Sandy was dead.

"Mr. Fitzgerald, I have to see you."

9.

SHE lived in a rent-controlled apartment in an old brownstone on West 56th Street, and her name was Leeta Kane. It's one of those streets where the kids still play stickball, and there's a bodega on the corner, with a storefront "Angelique Advisor" next to it. A block in any direction, and you can find luxury apartments renting for four or five times higher. But on this block, time stood still because the rents were frozen at 1950's rates. I found a New York Press parking zone on 57th Street and walked over to her place, passing Puerto Rican fritos and Greek fat sausages sizzling on grills and the joints selling pizza by the slice.

The name was scrawled on the mailbox in the hallway—Kane—4B. There are still four floor walk-ups. I huffed and puffed up, up, up, up, like somebody in *Barefoot in the Park*, until I finally stood before a green-painted door with a little peephole in the middle. I rang the bell and waited in the darkish hallway. The voice that came through the door was low and soft. "Who is it?" I identified myself. A chain lock clattered, and the door opened. "Hello, Mr. Fitzgerald."

She was what they used to call pleasingly plump, and her hair was no color that ever grew out of a human scalp in a natural state. It was somewhere between pink and orange. She was rather pretty in an unpretentious kind of way, with large, friendly brown eyes and artistically painted lips that were curved into a permanently inviting smile.

"Come in."

I stepped into the little apartment, which had a thrown together atmosphere about it. There was a low, round table with a glass top and under the glass were blown-up newspaper front pages.

"Sit down."

I sank into a billowy turkish divan. She sat beside me and lighted a cigarette with red-nailed fingers. She lifted her nice warm eyes to look at me through thick false eyelashes.

"I'm sorry I hung up on you the other time," said Leeta. "It really hit me between the eyes. Sandy dead!"

"It was in the paper."

"I don't read them very often. Just a lazy slob, I guess." She laughed hoarsely and with abandon. She wore a trim pair of slacks and a rainbow-striped top.

"How'd it happen?"

I told her the story of the hit-and-run car. She shook her head sadly.

"Just my luck," she sighed. "A nice guy, Sandy. Very nice. Shy and polite. And very understanding, you know what I mean? Give you the shirt off his back, Sandy would." She shook her head as though trying to fathom it. "Hit and run. Huh!"

"Did you know Sandy very long?"

Leeta exhaled smoke and shook her head. "Not so long. Less than a year. I went down to court to try to get some support money out of my ex-husband, you know what I mean?"

She stood and walked to the kitchenette, which was a sort of red-roofed pagoda sticking out of the corner of the room.

"You want a drink?"

"Sure," I said. "Got any beer?"

"Scotch? Vodka?"

"Scotch. Lots of water."

She made the drinks. Hers was a Scotch on the rocks. She lighted another cigarette and handed me the drink.

"My ex-husband was a one-out-of-ten type, you know what I mean? He'd send the alimony check one out of ten times." She laughed self-deprecatingly. "So, I had to go to the judge to get the court to goose him up a little. That's how I met Sandy. I had to file the court paper myself—they call it *pro se*—and Sandy showed me where to go and what to do. So, we had a drink."

I didn't have to ask Leeta a thing. She just kept on talking.

"My ex didn't exactly mend his ways, though. In fact, he upped and disappeared. Instead of one out of ten, it was none out of ten. Sandy? Well, he saw I was up against it. He started helping me out, you know what I mean?"

Another cigarette. Another splash of Scotch. I stood pat with mine.

"I don't want you to think I asked Sandy for money. I never did. He asked me to take him to some places—singles bars, that kind of thing. So I did. He'd never been out much I guess. Seemed to have a helluva good time. I guess he's got a wife, huh?"

"Yes. She lives in Larchmont, I think."

"I never asked." Her red lips formed a cave and smoke escaped slowly. "The thing is, Sandy never drank much at those places. Me? Sometimes I'd get paralyzed!" She laughed. "But not Sandy. So that's why I'm surprised he got tanked up and got himself run over."

"I'm surprised too, Leeta."

She looked at me uncertainly for a few moments. "You're a nice-looking man, Fitzgerald. What's your first name— Eddie?"

"Right."

She smoked thoughtfully, looking steadily at me.

"Sandy used to help me out, you know?"

"How much did he give you?"

"When he had it—a hundred bucks."

"How often?"

"Well, sometimes every week. Then maybe not for a week or two."

"Was the money in hundred-dollar bills?"

Leeta looked surprised. "Yeah. How'd you know that?"

"Well, he left some in his desk drawer."

Her eyes brightened. "He did?"

I could see at last where one of those bills was going to go.

"Did he say anything to you about where the hundreds were coming from?"

"Didn't ask, you know what I mean?"

"Know anything else?"

"Such as what?"

"Why anybody would want to kill him."

Leeta rocked back and then slowly leaned forward again. "He was killed?"

"I think he was."

She whistled. "Hey, wow! Friendly little guy like that."

"So is there anything else you remember?"

"Naw, nothing else. I just showed him around, you know, and he'd give me a hundred when he could. That's all. I never asked him for it, you understand."

"I understand."

She sat down on the divan beside me again, and put a soft hand on my hand. "I'm sorry, Eddie. Really." She smoked. "He was going to inherit some money, you know? He said he'd be able to help me out a lot when that happened."

"Inherit money?"

"That's what he said."

"How much? When?"

"I don't know. But he said it would be plenty." She looked at me wistfully. "I'm all alone now. You know what being alone is? It stinks, Eddie."

"I guess so."

"You go out much?"

"Well . . ."

"You want to kiss me?"

Leeta leaned over and held my arm with her hand, and brought her face up to me. I kissed her very gently. Her lips were soft and yielding. She leaned against me.

"It was nice with Sandy. I never was a problem to him. I wouldn't be a problem to you."

Well. At least I knew why she wanted to see me.

"You think you'd like to come and see me?"

"Leeta, I'll tell you the truth. You're a nice-looking lady, and you're good company. But I don't think so. Mainly, I couldn't afford it."

She took her head off my chest and straightened up. "It wouldn't be much. A hundred now and then."

I stood up. "If I could, Leeta—but I can't."

"Well." She sighed. "You going to leave me that last hundred, anyway?"

I opened my wallet, took out a bill, and handed it over. What the hell, it's what Sandy was going to do with it.

"Freshen that drink for you?"

I passed on that, and said I had to get going.

"If you change your mind . . ."

I went down the four flights a lot easier than I'd gone up, and walked along toward my car. So Sandy Pearl did have a girl on the side, and he was paying out $100 bills. And he was expecting some money—a lot of money—through an "inheritance."

I was getting somewhere, finally. But if Sandy Pearl was giving money to one woman, who was the other one—the stylish lady who had brought the bills to him at the court-house? It certainly wasn't Leeta Kane of the orange hair. And what had he been doing to get it?

I drove downtown, the image of Leeta Kane and her

smoky red mouth floating in my head. Funny, sometimes you do anything to get a girl: lie, boast, spend money like a drunken sailor. Then when one offers herself to you on a silver platter, you can't do it.

What a sap you are, Fitzboggen.

10.

How do you find someone who doesn't want to be found? That was the question repeating itself in my head. Where was Rita? Who was Rita? She had to be the one who brought those envelopes to Sandy Pearl. She was the only one I could think of who might be able to explain things. She had mentioned Tony. The only Tony I knew was Tony Kubek, and I didn't actually know him.

I remember one time a check forger decorated a good 40 blocks of midtown Manhattan with rubber, and he used the name of his old college roommate, who happened to have become an FBI agent by that time.

It occurred to me that a person making up a name would probably keep at least his first real one, since it would be too difficult to keep remembering a false first name. All that was necessary was to change the last name. Rita Jones or Smith had changed her last name to Meoli? Where would she get a name like that? Meoli must be the last name of somebody she knew. How could I find a somebody Meoli who knows a Rita who was once married to a Tony?

I got on the phone and started calling all the Meoli listings.

"Hello?"

"Hello? Listen, I'm trying to find Rita who was married to Tony, you know?"

"What?"

"You know a Rita who used to be married to Tony?"

"Tony who?"

"Well, I don't know."

"Who is this?"

New Yorkers are a very suspicious group, actually. Especially about phone calls. They always think some weirdo's on the line.

"I don't know their last name, but they're friends of the Meolis."

"Don't know 'em." The line went dead.

It was quite an intricate and clever ploy on my part, I thought. Except that it didn't work. I called all the Meolis in Brooklyn and not one of them knew any Tony who had been married to a Rita; and besides would I please go see a psychiatrist and stop with the phone fetish?

I called all the Meolis in Manhattan.

"What?" said one guy. "Tony and Rita? Where they running?"

"Running?"

"Who told you to call me?"

"Nobody."

"You trying to make a bet, there's no action here no more. I'm clean."

I laid the idea on Harry Reeves. His face went all wrinkled as though he'd just tasted a sour pickle.

"You know what you are, Fitzboggen? A plonk."

"A what?"

"You don't even know what a plonk is? That's ten pounds of crap in a five-pound bag." He went off into gales of idiotic laughter.

I retreated to my cubbyhole and called Lt. Dickson of Homicide.

"Look, do me a favor," Lt. Dickson said.

"What's that, Loot?"

"Nothing. Absolutely nothing!"

"Sorry, Loot, but strange cars keep trying to run me down."

A vast sigh came over the line. "Okay. I'll have Langner and Stevens call you."

"Do me a favor, Loot?"

"What?"

"Nothing. Absolutely nothing."

I went back to my telephoning, and kept at it most of the day between interruptions from Ironhead Matthews, who wanted to know when the hell I was going to do any work for *The Trib,* and from Reeves, who kept calling me a plonk.

Well, finally, late in the afternoon, this guy answered up in the Bronx.

"Is this Andrew Meoli?"

"This is him."

"Listen, I'm trying to locate a couple that I think are friends of yours—Tony and Rita."

"Tony and Rita Faso, you mean?"

I almost dropped the phone. "Yeah—Faso—that's them."

"They ain't married no more, you know. They usta be."

"Which one do you know?"

"Me? I know Tony. Used to, anyway."

My heart sank at that. "Not Rita?"

"Yeah, I know Rita, too. What do you want them for?"

"I'm a skip tracer for the Atlantic Insurance Company, and I've got to find Tony or Rita. They've been left some money in a will."

"How much?"

"Fifty thousand dollars."

"I think I know where Rita works. What's in it for me?"

Of course. "The company would probably pay a finder's fee."

"How much?"

New Yorkers are not only suspicious, they're greedy.

"I'm not authorized to say how much . . ."

The voice got edgy. "Well, I don't know then."

". . . but I'll guarantee you a hundred bucks."

The voice became friendly again. "I'll meet you. You give me the hundred; I'll show you where she works."

I ran over to Reeves's press room and asked him to cover for me.

"Now where you going—P.J. Clarke's again?"

"The Bronx."

"The *what!* What's going on?"

"It's not for the paper, so don't worry."

He looked at me with disgust. "Jesus!"

I went clickety-clickety-clickety up the FDR Drive in my Pinto pumpkin, up across the Triboro Bridge into the Bronx. Past the fire-blackened, abandoned apartments of the desolate South Bronx, where cannibalized auto skeletons lie in the streets like buildings in a war zone. On up the Grand Concourse, which was originally laid out as a copy of the Champs Elysées but is going seedy along with the rest of the borough.

The guy had said to meet him across from Yankee Stadium at a bar called Louie's. I drove up past the fortressy Bronx Supreme Court Building, then on to the new spiffy stadium, and saw Louie's. It's one of those neighborhood bars with leather booths along one side and the bar on the other, with blow-ups of Lou Piniella on the wall. At the bar, down at the end, sat a guy shaped like the hunchback of Notre Dame but without the hunchback. He sat there in a white dress shirt with no tie, drinking Heinekens. I walked over to him, and he searched my face for recognition.

"Andy?"

He nodded. "You the insurance guy?"

I said I was and slid onto the barstool beside him.

Andy looked like one of those street-wise drifters who don't work but who exist somehow, just as vultures and jackals live off the leavings of real predators. He had evasive eyes, an uncertain, quavering voice and a frequent nervous laugh.

"Some neighborhood," I said.

"Yeah. Used to be classy. Now . . ." He waved vaguely.

I lit a Tiparillo. He put a cigarette in his mouth and lit it.

"Rita works here in the Bronx?" I asked.

"You got the hundred?"

I took out a hundred-dollar bill and put it on the bar, under my hand. "I got it."

"Come on," he said.

We climbed into the Pinto and he directed me farther north up the Grand Concourse, all the way up to Fordham Road. Then we headed west to just past Jerome Avenue.

"Park here," said Andy.

He pointed to a bar just off the corner. The sign said McKean's.

"She works there," he said.

I got out of the car. "Let me go make sure it's the right Rita," I said.

"It's her. She used to be married to Tony Faso. It's got to be her."

I crossed to McKean's and went in. Andy hung back and looked through the window. It was a neighborhood Irish restaurant and bar, fairly deserted. The bartender looked up casually.

"Hi," I said.

"What'll it be?"

"Rita here?"

"Rita?" He seemed unconcerned.

"Rita Faso."

"Off tonight."

Just my luck. I looked around, and Andy was there, looking through the window anxiously. I waved him inside. He shook his head, but I waved him in again. He walked in, crossed over to me, and sat there trying to hide his face.

"What's the matter?"

"She's off tonight. You know where she lives?"

71

"Shoot," he muttered. "I know where Tony used to live."

"Show me."

"Shoot," he said. We left.

It was a second-floor apartment on West 184th Street, with a battered lobby and corridors smelling of boiled cabbage. Andy kept hanging back, but I wouldn't give him the money until I was sure. We took the jerky, scarred elevator up to the second floor and rang the bell. Nothing. I rang it again.

"You'll tell Tony I'm the guy who got the fifty grand for him, won't ya?" said Andy.

"I'll tell him." I rang the bell again. Still nothing. I tried the door handle, and to my surprise the door gave way. It opened.

"Rita?"

Nothing.

"Rita—it's me—Fitzgerald!" I stuck my head inside the doorway. Quiet. I stepped inside. A lived-in old Bronx apartment with a big, overstuffed sofa and a statue of Christ on the mantel. The radio was playing and a disc jockey was going on with his mindless banter. Into the living room, through the little dining room to the bedroom door.

She was on the bed, curled up, as though she had been sitting on the edge when it happened, and had just toppled over. There was blood in the corners of her mouth and in one of her eyes. Somebody had put a bullet through her left eye. Andy Meoli gaped, gasped, and threw up on the floor.

11.

WHEN a mess gets big enough, anyone who is anywhere near it finds out it's his fault. It's got to be somebody's fault, and if whoever did it can't be found then whoever can be found must have done it. The second murder—the third, as far as I was concerned—went off like a stick of dynamite in a domino factory. Everything started falling in every direction as soon as I telephoned the city desk.

"You've found *what?*" Ironhead Matthews was incredulous. "What the hell are you doing, Fitz? What are you doing up in the Bronx, anyway?"

Lt. Dickson of Homicide was more to the point when I got him on the phone. "Fitzgerald, have you hired yourself a lawyer?"

"What for?"

"Because everywhere you go, bodies fall out. Did I tell you to do nothing?"

"Yeah."

"But what did you do?"

"Nothing."

"You went out and dug up another body, goddammit!"

What was I supposed to say to that? I gave him the address and sat there watching Andy Meoli. Andy, whose approach to anything even vaguely unpleasant was a strong desire to be somewhere else—anywhere else—kept trying to sneak out of the apartment.

"I got these people mixed up with the other guys who run the pool hall, see? I don't know them."

"You're staying right here, Andy."

"You can keep the hundred bucks."

"Yeah," I said, "I can." That was the first decent development in months. "Look, Andy, what about Tony Faso?"

"Who?"

"Tony—who was married to Rita. Would he have done this?"

"How would I know?"

"Where is he?"

"Got me. I don't know. I gotta get outa here! I need a drink."

Could things get worse? Of course they could. And they did a few minutes later, when up the stairs walked Sherlock Holmes and Dr. Watson themselves.

"Where?" said big Dan Langner.

"In the bedroom."

Marty Stevens stuck his head in and looked. He came back.

"She's on the bed."

They had a firm grasp on the situation immediately. Marty Stevens got out his little notebook with the red cover and his ballpoint pen, and Langner fixed me with those hooded, unwavering eyes.

"What happened?"

Well, I told them everything I could remember about Rita Faso, and how I tracked her down in the Bronx through Andy Meoli. Andy sat in a deep, cushioned chair trying to transform himself into a turtle.

"She just walked into the courthouse looking for you?" said Stevens.

"As far as I can figure."

"How do you know she was looking for you?" said Langner.

Harry Reeves's leprechaun face and wry voice swam into my mind. "A hot brunette put the make on *you*, donkey?"

"Well, what else?" I said. "Why's a beauty like that come in out of the blue? Why'd she take me to bed?"

Marty Stevens's head bobbed up. "She took you to bed?"

"Well, I took her—she took me—we ended up together."

"Okay," said Langner. "We'll be in touch."

That's all they ever said.

"We can go now?" Andy appeared from the chair cushions and hunched forward like Bruce Jenner in the starting blocks at the Olympics.

"Not you," said Langner.

Marty Stevens stepped over to him and opened his notebook again. "Where's Tony Faso?"

"Oh, Jesus," whined Andy. "Oh, Jesus, Mary and Joseph."

Driving back down out of the Bronx, I decided that it was time to let Ironhead in on things. He had indicated a certain annoyance, and when Ironhead got annoyed people had a way of being assigned to the Brooklyn night police shack. When I walked into the city room, I could tell that the grapevine had picked up the fact that I was in some kind of a mess. For one thing, there were a couple of cops standing by Ironhead, and for another I could see Lt. Dickson of Homicide in the managing editor's office. And for a third, Danny the switchboard operator whispered, "Your ass is in a sling."

Ironhead glared at me and kept on glaring as I crossed the whole damn room. "Well, here he is at last—detective Fitzgerald!"

The big cop looked at me. "The Loot wants to talk to you." He walked away to the M.E.'s office.

"Come here," said Ironhead, leading me away into his office off the city desk. He closed the door. "What is all this about?"

"Ironhead, I'm telling you, as I told Lieutenant Dickson, somebody's trying to knock me off."

"Knock *you* off? Everybody else seems to be getting knocked off! Who's this Rita? They say you were banging her, and now she's dead."

"Banging her . . . ? Well . . ." News does get around in a murder case, doesn't it? "Not banging her—once, Ironhead! Look, she was trying to set me up."

"When are you going to make some sense?" His face was getting red and there was this throbbing vein in his forehead.

"Okay." I lit a Tiparillo. "Now, this is it. Somebody was paying off Sandy Pearl."

He was watching me unmovingly, unblinkingly.

"Sandy Pearl?"

"Somebody was giving him one-hundred-dollar bills for some reason."

"What reason?"

"That's what I've been trying to find out. Every time I get a lead on somebody, I go to see them and they turn up dead."

"That what's-his-name the ballplayer?"

"Arny Hayes." I nodded my head yes.

"And now this broad?"

I nodded again.

There was an insistent knock on the door. "Hey—the Loot's out here." The door opened. The cop stood aside. Lt. Dickson with his all-seeing eyes sailed in.

"Well, Mr. Fitzgerald. Who doesn't know how to take orders!"

Well, you never know in this world. All of a sudden, Ironhead shoves himself toe-to-toe and belly-to-belly and nose-to-nose with Lt. Dickson and starts screaming like a lawyer at a lying witness.

"Who told you to give orders to one of my reporters? Why isn't this man being given protection? When are you and your half-witted dicks going to find out who's trying to kill this man?"

Well, I'll tell you, I never thought I'd see Lt. Dickson back off, but I guess he wasn't used to anybody abusing him like that. The cop with him went half-white and seemed to be leaning forward as though fighting off a stiff wind.

"Mr. Matthews," Lt. Dickson replied when he got focused on Ironhead instead of on me, "I tried to give your man protection. I assigned two men to this case. I can't take your man's word that Sandy Pearl was murdered. There's no evidence. Just some idea he's got."

"What about Arny Hayes?" I said.

"As far as the department is concerned, that case has been disposed of."

Disposed of. What wonderful words the criminal justice system uses.

"What about Rita Faso?" I said.

"Yeah, what about her?" Lt. Dickson said. "That's what I want to know. How do you keep finding these dead bodies?"

I looked at Ironhead for help, and only then did I realize that he'd stopped talking. When I glanced at him, he was looking at me in a funny, dazed sort of way, half-frowning as though he'd gotten sidetracked.

"I'm taking him in," said Lt. Dickson.

Well, that snapped Ironhead back into context in a second. "You're taking who where?"

Now Lt. Dickson raised his voice. You could say he yelled. "He's holding things back!" He seemed downright frustrated. "We can't solve a puzzle when some of the pieces are missing!"

"You take him in, and you're getting the kind of heat that will put you back into the fucking Academy teaching police-shield polishing!"

"Wait a minute!" Somebody was interceding between

these two raging tigers, and I was surprised as hell to realize it was me. "Take it easy, for Chris' sake!"

"You shut up," Ironhead frothed. "You want Brooklyn night police?"

"Goddammit, keep him off police—we got enough trouble."

Well, it was a Chinese stand-off for a while, and there was a lot more yelling and badgering. I would be taken in as a material witness and thrown the hell into Rikers Island, said the Loot. And the Police Department would be nailed onto the front page with its pants down if that happened, screeched Ironhead. The Loot's aide-de-camp and I exchanged glances and kept our mouths shut.

Finally, it was decided that I would be brought down to the Manhattan district attorney's office with Ironhead and with a *Daily Tribune* lawyer and maybe with the M.E. and the publisher and who the hell knows who else, and I would then give a detailed statement under oath all about the entire, rotten, screwed-up mess, and if I or Ironhead or *The Daily Tribune* didn't like it there would be a goddam court order slapped on us so fast we would all think we were in the toilet! Well, it would take a court order and a subpoena and the State Court of Appeals to get a *Daily Trib* reporter into a goddam under oath, statement taking, third degree grilling, and if Lt. Dickson and the commissioner's office and the Presiding Justice of the State Supreme Court, First Department, and six other judges wanted to go to the mat on that they could just go the hell ahead!

It was all very polite, in other words, but nothing much got settled.

And then Lt. Dickson and his bodyguard and the two other cops were gone, sweeping out of the city room like a general after a battlefield consultation with the other side.

Ironhead Matthews stomped around his office kicking

the waste can and pounding on his desk. "Lousy pushy fuzz!" he raged.

"Yeah," I said.

And then he turned on me. His words came out like box-car type in a banner headline, all spaced out and black! "WHAT IS THIS ABOUT SANDY PEARL WAS MURDERED?"

"Huh?"

So that was what had stopped him in the middle of the conversation.

"Didn't I tell you about that?"

Now his words were soft—very soft—a strangled whisper.

"No. You didn't tell me. Tell me *now!*"

Well, I laid it all out for him. He sat there listening, immovable as an iceberg, glowering and making an occasional note. When I was finished, he looked up.

"So, you told Lieutenant Dickson that Sandy was murdered." He bent one of his fingers back.

"You told Harry Reeves of the *Post* that Sandy was murdered." Another bent finger.

"You told Hank the bartender Mazza." Bent finger three.

"You told dead Rita. I suppose you told the janitor and all those flowery pimps at P.J. Clarke's, and maybe you even told your idiot cat."

I was going to tell him I haven't got a cat, but it didn't seem like a good time.

"But you didn't tell your city editor." He smiled. I wondered how Brooklyn night police was as a steady occupation.

"Do you know what the district attorney's going to do to you when he gets you under oath? Are you aware of the fact that the story of Sandy Pearl being paid off will come out? Are you ready to hand that story over to Harry Reeves and the *Times* and the TV boys and radio? Is it your mission in life to shoot this newspaper down in flames?"

Ironhead lighted a cigarette and paced around like a tiger at the Bronx Zoo. Finally, he seemed to get an idea. "Shit!" he said. More pacing. Another idea. "Son-of-a-bitch!" Pace. Stop. "Hopeless!" He sat down.

"Goddammit, we can't let you go in front of the D.A. without figuring this thing out. If Sandy Pearl was on the take, we've got to find out before you tell those bastards anything."

"Right! See, that's what I was trying to do!"

"Shut up!"

Exactly.

"The first thing I want from you is a memo—a detailed, all-inclusive memo—about this whole screwed-up situation. I want everything from the top. Why would anybody pay off Sandy Pearl? Who was paying him? How much? Everything and anything."

"Right. As soon as I get back to the courthouse, I'll knock it right out."

"Courthouse?"

"You want me to write it here in the office?"

"You think I'd trust you back down there at the court-house?" Ironhead was indignant.

"But, this thing's in full flight."

"You're back on rewrite."

"But, Ironhead."

"No 'buts'! You don't stick your nose out of here. Don't you realize they'll have some goddam assistant D.A. looking for you with a subpoena?"

It's a fact of life in the newspaper business that people who can't be trusted to handle regular beats and write hard news get shoved into jobs where they can do the least damage—like being put on the desk someplace, or being made feature writers or columnists or something. That's why so many bosses tend to be numbskulls. They were put on the desk and kept getting moved out of the way until the next thing anybody knew they were all editors.

Somehow or other I got the damned memo finished, stuck the original on Ironhead's desk, and put a copy inside my jacket. I picked up an early paper and got on the elevator, looking at the pictures of Rita Faso on the front page. She was stylish, all right. John was right about that.

John?

My pumpkin went clickety-click down the FDR Drive as fast as I dared push it. I ran to the courthouse, up those Hollywood stairs, and was relieved to find John still in the information booth, checking the day's race results.

I went up to his glass booth and held up the pictures of Rita Faso on the front page.

John looked up, smiled, and glanced at them.

"Nice," he said. "Pretty. What a shame."

I searched John's face anxiously, looking for recognition in his eyes.

"That's her! Rita. The girl who used to bring those envelopes to Sandy," I said.

John looked again and shook his head.

"Naw," he said. "That's not her."

12.

I locked up my cubbyhole press room and walked across the vaulted lobby, bereft of ideas and tired of the whole thing. In my dejection I didn't even notice her at first and walked past before I heard her.

"I'm very sorry . . ."

It was the aristocratic blonde I'd spoken to earlier who had sailed past me like the QE-2. She stood in the courthouse lobby, hesitant, tentative, smiling at me in an uncertain way.

"Pardon me?"

"When you spoke to me the other day, I was so surprised I didn't know what to do."

"Sorry."

"No. It was rude of me." She held out her hand. "I'm Belinda Sharpe."

"Hello. Ed Fitzgerald. *Daily Tribune.*"

"Yes, I know." She smiled.

She was slim and tall and tantalizingly unusual, with the faint trace of an accent and a wistful, trembly quality. She seemed to look out at the world as though she were taking it on trial, suspending judgment for the moment. And yet there was strength and determination in her. She was uncertain, but launched into a struggle to overcome it, like someone coming back from an illness.

"What do you do?" I blurted out, in the way of pushy reporters.

"At the moment, I'm having a look around."

Left no opening, I mumbled something fairly idiotic about how historic and lovely the courthouse lobby is.

Which it is. But I'm afraid I was examining her rather immodestly, because she blushed.

"You have a case on?"

"No." No elaboration.

I was almost going to say, "Well, goodbye," because I couldn't think of anything else. But I said nothing and we both strolled toward the door. I followed her through the revolving doors out onto the great stone steps. She lingered, looking out over Foley Square, not in a hurry to walk away.

"The other day you invited me to have a drink," she said suddenly, not looking at me.

"Would you like to now?"

"I think I would," she said and her face was flushed again.

We walked down the long steps. She moved willingly, seemingly somewhat relaxing.

"Shall we walk up to Little Italy?"

She smiled with interest. "I'd like that."

Reporters tend to become gruff and unmannerly because they live in a system in which they must be abrupt. They cannot waste time on civilities because there is always a deadline hanging over them. But there was something about Belinda that put me off, caused me to speak more cautiously—a ladylike quality in her.

"Where are you from, Belinda?"

"Queens. Sunnyside."

We walked up Mulberry, crossing Canal Street, and stopped in a little Italian place that had a small bar in the front. She had white wine.

She looked around the little restaurant with lively interest, nodding her head and smiling and putting her hand on my arm when she spoke, and it was as though she were telling me she was enjoying herself.

"I'm quite surprised I'm here," she finally said.

"Why?"

"It's been a while."

She wore a blue suit that went well with her eyes, and a strand of pearls, and her blonde hair was short and natural. She was like someone who had been out of it for a few years. An enigma. A cultured mystery.

"So, how did I get so lucky?"

"What do you mean?"

"The other day you looked at me as though I were an insect. Today . . ."

She blushed again, very becomingly. "I do apologize for the other day. I was in a bit of shock then. You see, I'd just been divorced."

"Really?"

She smiled. "This is a sort of return to life for me."

"What do you do now?"

"That, indeed, is the question," she sighed.

Another beautiful lady at loose ends had turned up and seemed friendly. I don't know why it had taken me this long to become suspicious. Maybe because Belinda was a far better actress than Rita had been. Harry Reeves's jeering voice penetrated my consciousness: "A beautiful woman puts the make on a hump like you and you don't wonder what she's up to, Fitzboggen? Wake up!" I woke up.

This time, however, I would be more subtle. Belinda must get out of me whatever it was she needed to know. I would let her go about it in her own way. I did not want to find any more dead bodies.

We went on chatting pleasantly about casual things, about her apartment in Sunnyside, about her ex-husband, a professor who had moved to Virginia to teach in a private school. I kept waiting for her to pump me about Sandy Pearl. But this was a more cautious adversary. She must

84

have sensed my guarded mood. As it grew dark in Little Italy, she said she had to be going, and we walked down to Foley Square, where she got the subway. She would not hear of my driving her out to Queens, which did not surprise me. She lived in Queens, all right, the way I lived in Venice.

Belinda certainly didn't seem to be the type who would play this kind of a dirty game, and as I drove up the F.D.R. Drive, I began persuading myself that her interest in me had been totally personal. She was lonely. She liked me. What was so unusual about that?

I parked my car on East 82nd Street and was still thinking of the lovely Belinda Sharpe when my vision was intruded upon by two shapes moving toward me. They were both tall and dressed like Mafia hit-men, and I realized the beautiful Belinda had done her work well. I took off down East 82nd Street like Mookie Wilson chasing a fly to deep center field at Shea Stadium.

"Fitzgerald!"

So they knew me. I kept running to Second Avenue and then headed north. You know what? It's very difficult to run fast on a major avenue in New York City. There are too damned many people coming and going, not to mention delivery men carrying everything from suits to stacked cans of Libby's Jumbo Peas on two-wheeled trucks. I know, because I managed to avoid hitting the guy with the rack of suits in cleaners' bags only by creaming the guy pushing the Libby's Jumbo Peas. Down we went in a heap, with the Mafia hit-men on top of us. I sat up with a raging pain in my right shin and the face of the Mafia killer next to me.

The Murder, Incorporated, thug reached into his suit pocket and pulled out a gun. Only it looked just like a subpoena.

"You've just been served."

"Served?"

"Steadman. D.A.'s squad," he said.

I looked at the subpoena. It directed me to appear at the Manhattan district attorney's office at 155 Leonard Street at 10 A.M. in the forenoon on Thursday.

"Jesus Christ," I muttered. "Why didn't you say so?"

We all got up.

"You a cop?" The Libby's Jumbo Pea man howled.

"Yeah, yeah, it's all right," said Steadman.

"All right? I'm killed and it's all right? My merchandise is mobilized and it's all right? What's your name?"

"Henderson," said Steadman.

"Arrest this maniac!" he yelled, pointing at me.

"Okay!" Steadman-Henderson took my arm. "Let's go, you."

The other cop got up and took the other arm. "Let's go." We walked down Second Avenue and around the corner onto East 82nd Street. The Libby Pea man watched us with joy. "They pinched that screwball," he announced. "He's a mile high on junk!"

Everybody cheered. Probably never saw anybody get arrested before for anything in New York City.

"Look, Steadman, my city editor doesn't want me to accept any subpoenas."

"Too late."

"You're on the case now?"

"That's it," said the other detective.

"You're assigned to which murder?"

"Murder?" said Steadman.

"Arny Hayes or Rita Faso?"

The nameless detective smirked. "We're assigned to *you*, pal."

"Me?"

"Yeah. Where you go, we go."

"What about the Arny Hayes case?"

"Langner and Stevens."

Well, it sure was turning out to be a lovely day. All I had to do was walk into the *Trib* city room with Steadman and Nameless to make Ironhead Matthews extremely displeased.

"Coffee?" I suggested. They shrugged.

I went into a Chock-Full-O'-Nuts joint near the corner and they followed. Over a coffee and Danish, I laid it out for them.

"Look, fellahs. What you want from me with that subpoena, I could tell you."

"Is that so?" said Steadman.

"Then you wouldn't have to leave the subpoena with me. You'd have a full report on what I know, and everybody'd be happy."

"What *do* you know?" said Nameless.

I wish I could tell you that I did not do a dumb thing like take my copy of the memo out of my coat pocket and show it to them. I wish I could tell you that they looked over the memo, took the subpoena back, and departed. Did they do that? No, they did not. Steadman glommed the memo and slipped it into his pocket.

"Thanks."

"Don't mention it," I said. "Here's the subpoena."

Steadman put his hands in the air as though I were a leper reaching out to touch him.

"Uh, uh, uh. That's a legal paper."

"Wait a minute, Steadman. No subpoena, no memo."

They both got up. "The name's Henderson."

Nameless smiled. "I'm Steadman."

They walked out smiling. They had my memo. I had a subpoena. Ironhead would be more than displeased. He would be annoyed. I covered my face with my hands for a moment to stop things from reeling. When I looked up this crone with a pitted onion bulb between her eyes slid the check over to me and said, "Thank you."

I was so furious that I'm sorry to say I whispered hoarsely to her, "Why don't you go straight to hell!" She smiled and replied, "Not today," and walked away.

13.

You know how it is when you wake up and realize there is a flotilla of unpleasant problems sailing just beyond your consciousness? That as soon as you take that first sip of coffee you're going to remember some godawful mess you're in?

Marcus Aurelius advises: "Begin the morning by saying to yourself, 'I shall meet with the busybody, the ungrateful, arrogant, deceitful, envious, unsocial.' "

I took a sip of coffee, and it all came flooding back into my head. Belinda had set me up for those two Goliaths from the district attorney's squad. So what did that mean? Belinda was a cop? That didn't make sense. She was obviously spying on me for whoever was behind this whole thing, so how could she be a cop? It must have been just a coincidence that the Steadman Brothers nailed me after I left Belinda. Well, how did they find me? Possibly because I drive an orange Pinto that sounds like a wheat harvester? I was getting wonderful at asking myself questions. I just couldn't come up with any answers.

Once more I considered the possibility that the Sandy Pearl case existed only inside my fevered head. Maybe everything could be explained. Rita Meoli-Faso was an accident. Harry had given me one explanation for Sandy's money. His wife, Marcia, was cleaning up in TV commercials. Had she inherited money? Maybe that would clear up the whole matter for me. I called Danny the switchboard guy at *The Trib.*

"Danny? Fitz! Can you give me Sandy Pearl's home phone?"

"Ironhead's looking for you."

"Okay, okay," I said. "Sandy's home number."

Danny dug the number out of the staff file and read it to me.

"What's with Ironhead?"

"He's been over here three times asking for you. He's waving a sheet of paper around."

Terrific. My memo. There was the busybody already.

"I'll call later," I said.

"Where are you going?"

"Never mind."

I hung up and called Sandy Pearl's number. Marcia answered right away. "Hello?"

"Hey, Marcia, it's me—Ed Fitzgerald."

"Hi!" she said. "Nice to hear from you. I don't hear much from anybody from the office anymore."

"I saw your TV commercial. Great!"

"Really? You saw it?" She laughed. "It was fun."

"I hear you can really clean up with them."

The laugh subsided. "Clean up? On one commercial? Don't I wish I did."

We both fell silent, all small talk used up. "Listen, Marcia, I want to ask you something. About Sandy."

"Something about his pension? Are they going to increase it?"

"Well, no. I don't know anything about that."

"Oh."

"Marcia, I'm not trying to pry, but somebody told me you were pretty well fixed."

Marcia laughed sardonically. "They don't know me very well."

"Somebody told me you came from money and were going to inherit a lot more."

She was suddenly angry. "What? Are you trying to torment me?" She was crying.

"Aw, gee, Marcia . . . hey, don't!"

"I'm sorry. Fitz, I don't know what I'm going to do!

That one commercial and people think I'm fixed. Well, I'm not. I'm barely scrimping by. The kids are beginning to look like something out of the ghetto.''

So much for the tales of inherited wealth and TV riches.

"I'm sorry, Marcia."

"Well, I should be getting the pension. I may be able to go back to work soon. I'm sorry. In answer to your question, no, Fitz, I'm not an heiress. Sandy didn't by any chance leave a million bucks hidden away in that gopher hole office of his, did he?"

"No, just the hundred-dollar bills."

Why did I blurt that out?

"What?"

"I guess I'd forgotten to mention it."

"Forgotten hundred-dollar bills? How many? Were they Sandy's?"

"Yes, I guess so. Four of them. Look, I'll send them to you."

"Four hundred dollars? Oh, Fitz, you're a lifesaver. My god, I love you to pieces! You don't know what this means to me."

Well, I was beginning to feel pretty good about the bad feeling I was having about giving up the four hundred bucks, when Marcia said, "Why haven't you told me about this before?"

"Uh, well . . . I forgot."

"Forgot? He forgot! How do you like this? I'm walking around on my heels without stockings and my kids are living on hot dogs and he forgets hundred-dollar bills! Irresponsible, stupid, uncaring . . . bachelor!"

"I'm sorry."

"Sorry! Leave the money for me in an envelope at the office. I'll pick it up. And I thought you were a friend of Sandy's!" Crash! Silence. Well, there was the ungrateful one.

As I drove clickety-clickety-clickety to the office, I realized that the vain hope I'd had that there was nothing to the whole thing had once more vanished. The $500 remained unexplained, and worse, I was about to give the last of it away.

When I got off the elevator, I put the four big ones into an envelope and gave them to Theresa at the reception desk. "Marcia Pearl will be by to get this," I told her.

I headed reluctantly toward the city room, my head echoing with possible conversations that would overwhelm me. Ironhead would come stomping over with that damned memo and start raging that I'd shot the paper down in flames. Or Charles W. Corcoran, the company lawyer, would come over and sit down in that somber insurance-man way of his and look just over my left shoulder while talking soothingly of what I shouldn't do.

"I wouldn't go near the courthouse, Fitzgerald. They'll serve you with a subpoena. If they try to do that, contact the legal office."

"I already got served with a goddam subpoena by two treacherous Mafia killers."

Now, there is a look for you—the funeral, down-in-the-mouth, pitying stare of newspaper counsel Charles W. Corcoran when you tell him something that is even remotely dangerous to the paper.

They were the other ones Marcus Aurelius had warned me to expect—"the arrogant, deceitful, and unsocial." It depressed me so much that my feet halted when I went past the library.

"Could I have the clippings of Sandy Pearl's by-line stories?"

Marvin, the library guy, brought me a fat envelope full of them. I looked at the sheaf of stories and wondered if there might be an answer there somewhere.

Then, the howling started in my imagination again. I knew damned well Ironhead and Corcoran would try to keep me in the office so I wouldn't get a subpoena. And what would happen when I told them I already had one?

"What?" Ironhead would shriek.

"Unfortunate!" Corcoran would say frowningly to a spot on the wall.

They were still going on like that inside my head as I took the elevator back downstairs, got into the pumpkin, and headed on down the F.D.R. Drive. They'd find out soon enough that it was too late to worry about my getting a damned subpoena. Besides, I didn't dare get stuck in the office.

14.

When I got to my cubbyhole press room, the phone was ringing and ringing as though there were a handful of angry hornets inside. Miltie looked up and smiled, as always, and I whispered to him, "Answer that for me, will you, Miltie? And tell me who it is."

He picked up the phone. "Hello?" He listened. "Who's calling?" He looked at me inquiringly. "The office?"

I involuntarily flinched, and Miltie said, "No, he's not here. Okay, if he shows up, I'll tell him." He hung up. "The office."

"Thanks," I said.

"What's cooking?" he asked.

"Pastafazoul," I said, and sat down with the stack of Sandy Pearl's by-line stories. I started reading them. Divorce cases, damage suits, negligence suits, judgments, jury verdicts, show-cause stories, politicians' suits, taxpayers' suits, a litany of private and public woes. This attorney, that attorney, Bernard Weinberg and Mickey Silberman, Adolph Menjou Berg, Charley Rooney, Mickey Silberman and Mickey Silberman again.

More and more, the name of Mickey Silberman popped up in the kind of flashy divorce and negligence story that didn't really require the mention of a lawyer, but which would be likely to get that lawyer the kind of publicity that would lead to more clients.

Mickey Silberman? A pattern? Was he the one that was paying off Sandy Pearl? Mickey Silberman who defended wilted Playboy bunnies against vile stockbrokers? Mickey Silberman who had been kicking Edward Weinberg in the crotch for 25 years? Rita had been involved in getting a divorce. So had Belinda. Was Mickey sending his clients after me?

I got on the phone and called Mickey Silberman's office, and in a moment he was on the line, all affable charm and ooze. Could I talk to him? Absolutely. When? Any time. Now? Now.

"I'm going to be in Giambone's for lunch," I said.

"Half an hour?"

"Okay." I packed up the clippings. "Thanks, Miltie," I said, and went out the door.

I hopped across the hall and stuck my head in the other press room. Harry Reeves looked up and whooped. "Well, if it isn't the Plonker."

"Hello, you tabloid hack."

"Hey! I saw a pretty fancy floosie hanging around your press room the other day. I think she was looking for whore's court."

"What do you know about Mickey Silberman?"

"It's with a 'b' not a 'v.' "

"Was he a good friend of Sandy Pearl's?"

Reeves's eyes rolled in his head. "Ahhhhh, good god a'mighty!"

"Listen, they've subpoened me, so don't tell me it's all a crock."

"Subpoened you?" Reeves looked concerned. "Listen, they want to take you over to Beekman Downtown Hospital and put you on a sex appeal measuring machine to see if you can or can't get a rise out of a Times Square bag lady, see? Well, my advice is don't let them. Bag ladies ain't that hard up yet."

And there you see what happens when you put an important fact in front of a psychopathic orangutan.

I was out in the corridor, starting to head through to the back door, when Miltie came out of my press room and waved at me. "Al Wagner called. From Surrogate's

95

Court." I made a mental note to call Wagner, and then headed through the great rotunda and down the elevator. Out the back door of the courthouse, across through the Chinatown playground to Mulberry Street and Giambone's.

Several regulars were already there, electing and destroying the political establishment in martini glasses. I sat at a table and ordered a Schaefer and in walked Mickey Silberman, round and pink and blue in double-knit polyester. He sailed right over to my table and took a chair.

"There you are!" Mickey Silberman waved his arm and Angie the waiter scurried over. "Apolinaris!" snapped Mickey, and Angie hopped to it. I've always wanted to be able to do that, you know? Order some fancy Greek liquor or whatever it was and have waiters jumping because they knew I knew what I was doing.

"Well," smiled Mickey. "How's the courthouse?"

"Oh, fine, Counselor. If I could ever figure out what was going on."

"Your stories are all wonderful. You seem to know your way around." He smiled. Hang around lawyers enough when you're covering the courthouse and you get to know what it's like to be a nice-looking girl who's always being propositioned. A courthouse reporter cannot tell a bum joke to a negligence lawyer.

Angie put the Apolinaris in front of Mickey. It appeared to be a sparkling Greek white wine. He poured, sipped, waited.

"You knew Sandy Pearl, right?"

"Certainly."

"He wrote you up a few times."

"A wonderful writer."

"Always spelled your name right, I guess."

Mickey's professional face went into a little unhappy spasm. "Well, Sandy was not the greatest speller. He got it wrong a few times."

96

"Counselor, I don't know how to ask you this. It's what you lawyers would call a leading question."

"Ask away. You're among friends."

"Mickey, I'm not satisfied with what they say about Sandy Pearl's death. I don't think it was an accident."

Mickey didn't blink.

"Something stinks. Either Sandy was onto a big story that somebody didn't want printed, or somebody was paying him off, or I don't know what."

Now Mickey blinked. He poured more of that sparkling white Greek wine.

"I'm trying to find out if the guy who was paying him off is the guy who got him run over."

Mickey drank deep of the Apolinaris.

"The thing is, counselor, it's getting out of hand. The Manhattan D.A.'s office has subpoened me. They're going to put the screws to me."

"Angelo!" Mickey Silberman's hand waved. Angie hopped over. "Dewar's." Angie hopped away.

Mickey Silberman took off his rimless glasses and polished them like a maniac.

"What are you going to tell the D.A.?"

"I don't know, Counselor. What would you suggest?"

"Are you going to bring me into it?"

"Counselor," I said, "I'd be very happy not to mention you at all."

A long, legal sigh. "I never gave Sandy any payoff." He closed his eyes, opened them. "I fixed him up with a couple of girls, that's all."

That tic in his cheek was back.

"We went out a couple of times with broads and I picked up the tabs. Now, that's it!"

"Was this going on right up until he died?" I asked.

"What? No-oo! What are you talking about? We hadn't been out in a year. This is all ancient history."

"What happened? Fix him up with a dog?"

"I don't know," he said. "He stopped using my name in his stories." A bitter little grin came over his mouth and eyes. "Maybe he got a better offer."

I walked back to the courthouse completely disgusted. If Mickey Silberman wasn't my man, who was? It had seemed so perfect. A lawyer who handled divorces. Rita, a divorcée, had come after me. Then Belinda, another divorcée. A divorce lawyer who was always around the courthouse was the perfect quarry. But it wasn't him.

I came in the lobby and heard the faint clicking of heels in the rotunda. That elegant walk. Belinda Sharpe was walking through the great rotunda toward the elevators. She was chatting away animatedly with someone. They got into the elevator and the door was closing when he turned enough for me to see it was Bernard Weinberg.

15.

ONE was shortish with faded blond hair and a perpetual, amiable grin, like Morey Amsterdam in his better days. The other was dark with a pug face and a lantern jaw like Raymond Burr.

"Harry Coutros," said the pug face. "This is Carroll Roberts."

More detectives in my press room. Once I couldn't get arrested. Now there were three sets of cops crowding me.

"Now, look, Fitzgerald," said Coutros, "how about helping us out, huh? Let's make this easy on each other, huh?"

Carroll Roberts gave me an amiable Morey Amsterdam grin and asked for one of my Tiparillos. "Mind?" he said. "I'm shameless."

I lighted his Tiparillo. "What case are you on?"

"Rita Faso."

"What about Langner and Stevens?"

"Arny Hayes."

"How about Henderson and Steadman?"

"Who?"

Detective Roberts smiled. "Henderson and Singleton. They both call themselves Steadman sometimes. Breaks up the day."

Coutros had a little notebook out and was going over it with a pen, checking things off.

"Deceased died of a .22 caliber bullet wound through the left eye. Same weapon that killed Arny Hayes."

I looked at him. "What?"

"Same weapon."

You might not believe this, but that was the first time it

really came home to me. A chill went through my chest and up my neck.

"The same gun?"

I knew it was the same gun, of course. It had to be. But this made it official. It really linked things up in a series of murders. Somebody was out there with a gun killing people as I tried to find them. Hit and run was sort of questionable, but not two people dead from the same .22 caliber weapon.

Well, they grilled me about Rita Faso. How long had I known her? Had I had "relations" with her—what a goofy word. What, if any, connection did she have with Arny Hayes? What about Tony, her ex-husband?

"You got me," was my answer to most questions.

And then Coutros and Roberts stood up together. Coutros made a somber Raymond Burr face and flapped his little notebook shut.

"We'll be in touch," he said.

Where had I heard that one before?

They walked out.

The phone rang. I looked at it, and realized that Ironhead was probably trying to track me down. I conjured up a bizarre Brooklyn accent to use on him.

"Hallo?"

"Is that you, Teddy?" The guy was breathing hard and trying to get an answer in a hurry.

"Who do you want—Teddy?"

"The *Daily Tribune* reporter?"

"Eddie."

"You asked about the Amster case?"

It was my old friend Al Wagner at Manhattan Surrogate's Court.

"Yes, Al."

"It's back on the calendar, Teddy," he said. "I'm watching it for you."

"Good."

"What about the opera tickets?"

"The what?"

"I keep calling to ask you, but you're never there. Can you get *La Traviata?* Or if not, *La Forza Del Destino?*"

"You mean the Met?"

"Mr. Pearl said he'd get me opera tickets."

"How many?"

"Three. Or if you can get them, five. Any night. I'll let you know when the Amster case is on for disposition. I'd rather have *La Traviata.*"

"Okay. What's the Amster case about?"

"Oh, I can't go through all these cases, Teddy. It's hundreds of pages. Been here forever."

"Sandy Pearl was watching it?"

"He told me to let him know, and he'd get me tickets. I hope it's with Luciano Pavarotti."

"Okay, Al. Keep in touch."

"Talk to you later, Teddy."

I went back through the great rotunda to the rear elevator, rode down into the basement and went looking for Billy in the county clerk's office. Another one of those thunderingly obvious facts that I'd overlooked had struck me. The two messengers who had been sent after me were both divorced women. I had forgotten that divorce cases are filed separately, not with the other civil cases. They have their own series of index numbers.

Billy smiled at me. "Where you been, Fitz? What's doing?"

Good old Billy. Hadn't heard a word about my nefarious doings. Or didn't care.

"Nothing much, Billy. Hey, could you check a divorce case for me? Rita versus Anthony Faso. Must have been last year."

"Faso versus Faso? Okay. Is it a hot one?"

"I don't know, Billy."

"Okay. You getting me Golden Gloves tickets this year? Sandy always got us Gloves tickets."

"Sure, Billy. How many?"

"Ten."

"*Ten?* For Chris' sake, who goes?"

"Everybody."

I was confident that Faso versus Faso would be the elusive index number Sandy Pearl had left to bedevil me. It wasn't long before Billy was back to say there was no Faso versus Faso divorce case in his records.

"But Billy, I know she got a divorce."

"Not in this court, she didn't."

No record in Manhattan State Supreme Court? Of course not! Rita and Tony lived in the Bronx, where a whole different set of index numbers would be found.

I called our reporter, Al Fayette, at the Bronx Supreme Court Building up near Yankee Stadium and got him to check out Faso versus Faso for me at the clerk's office there. It took a while, but eventually he got back to me.

"It's here," said Al. "Looks routine. What do you want to know?"

"The index number, Al. It's 2381, am I right?"

"Naw, that's not it," said Fayette. He read off the number but it wasn't 2381. The elusive Index Number Sandy Pearl had left me did not refer to the divorce case of Faso versus Faso.

I sat in my little press room cursing the idiot day I'd spent to no avail. Not only had I met the ungrateful, and the arrogant, I'd met the greedy and the grasping. Ten Golden Gloves tickets. And opera tickets! Al Wagner wanted opera tickets? I decided to go to Surrogate's Court and find out what that was all about.

16.

THERE was a time back in the 1800's when New York went through this Egyptian building phase. They put up a city jail patterned after a pharaoh's tomb. Naturally, everybody started calling it "the Tombs." When they tore that jail down and built the present one next to the Manhattan Criminal Court Building, people called the new jail the Tombs, too. Well, Manhattan Surrogate's Court must have been designed during the Egyptian craze, because it's also something like a huge, marble tomb.

It's one of these ornate, palatial buildings with quaint carved statues of Peter Stuyvesant and Father Knickerbocker up on the roof gazing down benevolently upon justice-seekers. The lobby has a fine Egyptian ceiling full of cat gods, and in each corner is a black globe upon which a black, glaring eagle is perched. It's really a marvelous museum of a place, with a ponderous marble staircase. In the wood-carved and marble courtrooms, they still have big fireplaces, as though the rooms were something out of Citizen Kane's mansion.

Anyway, I searched around the gilded, elaborate old ruin until I found the probate clerk's office on the fifth floor, and looked up Al Wagner. He turned out to be a graying, tall and thin old guy with glasses, wearing a gray sort of suit that faded into the background, and he was jumpy and nervous. You had this feeling that he couldn't pause for a second, because there were endless stacks of musty old wills piling up somewhere, waiting to be indexed and filed and entered in ledgers.

"Oh, hello there, Teddy," he said when I introduced myself.

"Ed," I said. "Ed Fitzgerald." For once and for all, I wanted to get that straightened out.

"Oh," said Wagner. "I've just been talking with the State Supreme Court reporter—Teddy. Are you taking his place?"

It was no use.

"I tried to tell Teddy that the Amster Case is on the calendar again, and that it's going to be disposed of in a few days now."

"What *is* the Amster Case?"

Al Wagner looked very unhappy, and checked the gray, red-spined ledger in his hands. "Oh, Mr. Fetzer, I can't dig into all those pages."

"Well, why was Sandy Pearl so interested in it?"

"I don't know that, Mr. Fetzer. He just came looking for it one day."

"Show me."

Wagner's eyes swam behind his glasses. "It's on the calendar Thursday. In the courtroom."

"Couldn't I look it over now?"

"Well, but the papers are sealed."

"They're public documents, aren't they?"

"They are. Unless they've been ordered sealed. You can hear all about it when they get to court."

"You said it's hundreds of pages?"

"Oh, my, yes! Two or three feet thick."

"Well, how am I going to know what's going on in court if I haven't gone over the papers in advance?"

Wagner stood there, wavering and rubbing the ledger.

"They don't like anybody to look at sealed papers. They're very fussy about that."

"Wagner," I said, "don't tell me you've never shown sealed papers to anybody. Didn't Sandy Pearl look at them?"

"Yes," said Wagner. "I think that's why they were sealed."

"Look," I coaxed, "I just need to see them for background. I won't use anything that doesn't come out in open court."

"Well . . . I could get in dutch!"

It was a rotten thing to do, I admit, but I couldn't stand there playing cat-and-mouse all day. "Wagner, I'm having a helluva time getting those Met tickets. They're costing me fifty bucks apiece."

Some kind of muttered response came out of him—"Oh well, oh dear!" He sort of shuffled off, out of the clerk's office, looking back at me. I followed. He led me around and down a hallway to a frosted-glass door, and held it open until I slipped inside. He stepped in after me. The room was filled with a crazy, cramped array of pull-out files and expandable cardboard envelopes. He went behind a counter and opened a filing cabinet and brought back four bulging, brown legal files. He carried them with both hands and laid them on a green table for me.

"There," he said. "Go through them as quickly as you can, now. I'll be in a jam if they find out."

"Fast as I can," I said.

"I'll be back," he said, and hurried away, the curator of a museum of entombed mummies.

I looked at the first thick, brown cardboard envelope and all of a sudden there it was jumping out at me—the missing index number—2381/21. No wonder I couldn't find it. The case dated back to 1921. The estate of the late, late, late Sheldon Amster. I opened the first sheaf of whereases and wherefores and plunged in.

I hate to tell you what it's like reading a closely reasoned, carefully legalized estate file. Everything is repeated over and over again, and buttressed with all these "on information and beliefs" and "deponent is sworn and deposes" and what-have-you.

I sat there for two hours reading the saga of the Amster family, which went all the way back to colonial times, when Johannes Amster operated the White Swan Inn near the Battery on the stagecoach route to Boston and Philadelphia and westward into the wilds of Pennsylvania. Johannes, who had emmigrated from Holland as a boy, got rich by provisioning the city and state governments with everything from rum to beef to muskets. And where Johannes left off, his son Frederick continued, adding a lively trade in Holy Bibles to the Amster business.

The Amsters provided muskets and gunpowder and "provision of beef and corn" to all sides in the French and Indian war, it appeared, and did the same for the British and the upstart United States of America. They seem to have made their first fortune out of the Revolutionary War. Then came August Amster, who used the family connections to swing beef and armaments contracts with the U.S. government during the Civil War, and quadrupled the already handsome family fortune.

Then came Sheldon Amster, born in 1847. Sheldon had found religion somewhere in his middle years and apparently got out of the boisterous and chancy beef provisioning and armaments businesses and was content to amass a fat portfolio of stocks and bonds, along with several banks and a good slab of Manhattan real estate.

There were his assets, all totaled up in monotonous columns: 60,000 shares of common stock in Sears, Roebuck, another 200,000 in the Wallace Ore Transportation Company, shares of I.T.&T., Minnesota Mining and Manufacturing, United Airlines, United Fruit. Then the real estate: the Rudy Building on Columbus Circle, the Schmidt-Amerson Apartments, land in mid-Manhattan, land in Queens.

All very interesting, but nowhere could I find a clear total of what the estate was worth.

I jotted down as much of the basic stock holdings and real estate as I could. It had to be worth millions, I figured. More than most ink-stained newspaper wretches make in a month.

Still, I didn't see what made the estate so fascinating. There are lots of dead millionaires in Manhattan. Maybe it was the list of heirs, I finally decided. I plowed through more papers and finally realized that there were no heirs. Sheldon Amster had died a bachelor, with no legal heirs, in 1921. And a couple of feet of court papers spelled out the strenuous battles that had been going on ever since over who should get his estate.

Three banks that were, in effect, owned by the estate had fended off various challengers who turned up claiming to be either legal issue or bastard kin of the Bible-thumping dead bachelor. Conservators had been appointed and reappointed and replaced. Legions of lawyers had come and gone. But the estate lay there, stubbornly refusing to get settled, and there appeared to have been very little activity concerning it for the last few years.

It was as though the fabulous treasure of Captain Kidd had been buried beneath the courthouse and there it lay in a legal paper deep, waiting for someone to discover a way to extricate it.

I was sitting there, lost in thought, puffing on a Tiparillo when Al Wagner came scurrying in carrying another stack of briefs. He looked at me and halted, as though stunned by an electric cattle prod.

"Smoking? Oh, good lord, Mr. Fester, you can't smoke in Surrogate's Court!"

"Sorry," I said, and stubbed out the cigar. "Listen, Al, what happens to an estate when there are no heirs?"

He was already shoving the papers into their final resting

place in a metal filing cabinet, and he talked to me over his shoulder. "If nobody claims it, it goes to the State of New York."

"The state gets it?"

"Yes."

No wonder the papers were more than two feet thick. All that money about to disappear down the undeserving public drain.

"I can't figure out what the estate's worth," I said.

Wagner walked over reluctantly and looked at the first paper, the original probate petition. He turned it over, and scribbled on the back was the notation, "1,000 plus."

"Over a million," he said.

"How much over?"

"Oh, we don't go into that. If it's over a million, that's all we indicate."

"How can I find out?"

"Well, the lawyer could tell you."

The lawyer. I hadn't even checked to see who it was. I looked at the letterhead. Bernard W. Weinberg.

"He's a big lawyer," said Wagner. "Handles a lot of cases."

"So I've heard."

"I have to go. Are you almost finished?"

"Almost."

"I thought you only wanted to know when the case would be in court," Wagner fussed. "I didn't know you were going to come down here and root around like this. This is very bad. What are you looking for?"

"Well, I'll tell you, Al, something's not kosher, you understand? Somebody's playing games here."

Al Wagner shook his head in agitation, and another "oh, my," popped out. He scurried away between the files. I plunged back into the legal maze. According to the papers, the battle over the estate had raged with intensity in the twenties, when challenger after claimant came forward to claim it, only to be met with a blizzard of opposition papers from the State of New York and from attorneys representing banks, trusts and stockholders. The papers had grown increasingly fewer in recent years, and nothing at all had been filed for about ten years.

Then, about a year and a half ago, another claimant had surfaced. A legal affidavit declared that one Maria Amster, a distant cousin of Sheldon Amster, had come forth and had dutifully claimed the estate. Maria declared that a distant relative of hers and a distant relative of Sheldon's were brothers back in Amsterdam in the 1600's. While one brother, Johannes, went to New Amsterdam, a grandson of the other brother had emigrated to Philadelphia. Eventually one of the Philadelphia Amsters, W.B. Amster, had moved westward to Kansas, where the family line had been lost.

But now, after all those years, Maria Amster of Topeka, Kansas, claimed to be descended from the lost W.B. Amster. Unlike other claimants, Maria had documents and an impressive sponsor. She was able to show that in the 1880's there was among the congregation of the Dutch Reformed Church in Topeka, Kansas, her great-grandfather William Amster, who had been a church deacon. Her court papers maintained that the lost W.B. Amster and her own great-grandfather William were one and the same person. Therefore, the estate was rightfully hers as the only living heir.

The prime exhibit of her petition was an affidavit signed by the current pastor of the Dutch Reformed Church of Topeka, the Reverend Martin Schuyler, certifying that W.B. Amster was in fact William Amster.

The affidavit had been properly sworn to, stamped by the court clerk, and admitted into evidence by Judge Foley. A period of 90 days had been set for any challengers who might come forward to contest Maria's right to the estate.

The 90 days were up Thursday. No opposition papers were on file in the huge stack.

One final paper lay there. It directed that the Amster estate be transferred to Maria Amster Taylor in care of the Banque de Suisse Nationale in Geneva, Switzerland.

I'm afraid I forgot about Wagner's admonition not to smoke admist all those musty documents, and lighted up. It certainly was a fascinating case. Almost ninety days had gone by without a single challenge to this claim. Sheldon Amster's fortune would finally slip quietly out through the back door of Surrogate's Court into a numbered Swiss bank account.

No wonder Sandy Pearl had been so interested in the case.

Wagner came careening into the room again, with more papers, blinking from behind his glasses in the semi-gloom of the filing room.

"Finished?"

I closed up the stack of papers. "I guess so."

"It'll all be clear in court Thursday."

"I'll bet."

"Is it a good story?"

"It's beautiful."

"Don't forget the tickets. And be careful with that cigar, please."

As I walked through the gloom of the lobby, I had the feeling everything was on the tip of my tongue, but I still couldn't sort it out. Sandy Pearl was watching the Amster Case. What the hell? He was watching a dozen others, too. But there was something not right about this one. What was it?

And then I spotted them coming into the building together, chatting away amiably—Belinda Sharpe and Bernie Weinberg. They were so wrapped up in each other they didn't see me. Beautiful Belinda was earning her fee, all right.

Back up through Foley Square to my little press room, where I called Marvin in the *Daily Trib* library.

"Marv? Fitzgerald."

"What's up, Fitz?"

"Would you see if we have anything on Sheldon Amster?"

"Amster? Did you find another stiff, Fitz?"

"Not this time, Marv. Sorry. This one died in 1921 and left a lot of bread."

"Amster?"

"And see if there's anything on a Maria Amster or a Maria Amster Taylor."

"Hold on."

When he came back on the line he said, "Fitz? Nothing on Maria. Plenty on Sheldon Amster. Big case in the twenties and thirties. Four fat envelopes."

That was Marv's way of telling me he wasn't going to dig through all that for me on the phone.

"Oh. Well, when was the last story?"

More papers rustled. "Looks like about nineteen forty-eight."

"Nineteen forty-eight? Nothing since then?"

"Don't see anything."

"No recent stories at all?"

"Nope."

Despair welled up in me. The Amster case had to be what Sandy's death was all about, I kept telling myself. But he wasn't writing about it. If somebody had been paying him off to get the story in the paper, they hadn't been getting their money's worth.

17.

SWITCHBOARD people at newspapers are combination snoops and buttinskis, if you want to know, because they are always tracking down reporters when they aren't asking brazen questions of people who call up the paper. Either they doubt anonymous callers who say they're going to blow up the World Trade Center, or they find reporters who are secretly shacked up at the Statler-Hilton with stewardesses and ask them to cover a fire that has just broken out in the hotel.

I was still adrift in my stupor when the phone started doing a tarantella around my desk. Miltie, the *Women's Wear Daily* guy, raised his eyebrows when I glanced over at him. It was his way of asking if he should answer for me. I said go ahead. He came over and picked up the phone.

"Hello?" Miltie said, and that was the only actual word he got out, because all the other sounds were "uh-huhs" and "yeahs" and "uhhs." He handed the phone to me.

"Take a message," I tried to mouth silently, but he shook·his head and kept sticking the phone at me.

"They know you're here," he said.

My mistake had been making a call from the press room to Marvin in the library. When I did that, a little light went on on the switchboard, and Danny knew I was there. So I had to take the phone, and Danny told me that Ironhead had told him that if I didn't get right up to the city room *tout de suite* I would be sorrier than that Weatherman in Greenwich Village who blew himself up with his own bomb. I realized that·perhaps I had better put in an appearance.

When I came off the freight elevator, Ironhead was already out of his office dodging chairs to get to me. I felt like Anna Leonowens in *Anna and the King of Siam* when the

112

king came vaulting toward her chirping, "Who? Who? Who?"

"Where the hell have you been?"

Sometimes I wonder why I didn't join the fire department like my Uncle Phil Roura.

Well, nothing would do but that Ironhead and I had to go into his office and close the door so he could chew me out. I was more or less dragged across the room, past the city desk and the switchboard—where Danny the operator sat shaking his head as if to say, "I told you so!"—past the copy boys' bench where the copy boys and girls sat staring away from us in terror, past Chuckie the Nut Call Editor who pretended to be oh, so busy, but who was watching us every step of the way—into Ironhead's office. Wham! The door shut.

"Sit down there!"

I sat.

Pace around behind the desk. Lift up the memo. Look at it as though it were a murder indictment. Glare at me over the top of the memo. Lay the memo down.

"I don't know where to start! I don't know where the goddam hell to begin with you!"

"It's a mess, all right."

"What?"

It wasn't really what you'd call a question. It was sort of a molten shout that meant approximately, "Shutthehellup-yougoddamidiot!"

He picked up the memo again. "Where's the five hundred bucks?"

"Five hundred bucks?"

"You say in your memo that there was five hundred bucks in Sandy Pearl's desk! Where is it?"

Oh, *that* five hundred bucks.

"Uh . . . let me think now . . ."

113

That vein in Ironhead's forehead stood out and started to throb.

"You have to think about it? How many five hundred bucks have you got to worry about?"

"Marcia Pearl's got it."

"You gave evidence to Marcia Pearl?"

"Well . . ."

"Why?"

"She says she's out of stockings."

Something on the wall seemed to suddenly fascinate Ironhead. He stared at a spot for a minute or two. Then he let his breath out and said in a whisper, "*Stockings?*"

You might not believe this, but even as I sat there getting chewed out, bits and pieces were whirring around in my head. It was like a slot machine where the wheels spun and one stopped on a pear, and then the second one went errrrrrra-thump! And it was a second pear. And then the third one went errrrrrra-thump!—and it was a plum. Where the hell was that third pear?

"Or is it a bell?"

"What?" Ironhead looked at me crossly. "What bell?"

"It's what's missing, Ironhead. The third pear."

"Pear?"

"Sometimes it's a pear, sometimes a bell."

"Fitzgerald, you've got to start talking clearly. We're in the damned communications business."

"It's all in the memo, Ironhead. There's Sandy Pearl getting hundred-dollar bills from somebody. Some nice-looking woman is bringing him the dough. He's giving the hundreds to Leeta Kane . . ."

"I thought you said Marcia Pearl."

"That was later."

"Later . . . ?" Ironhead grabbed the memo. "I want to know if Sandy was being paid off!"

"I think so."

Ironhead lowered the memo. His head leaped out at me like a badger's, and he seemed upset. "You *think* so? Goddammit, was he or wasn't he?"

"Somebody was giving him hundred-dollar bills, it looks like."

"Who?"

"Some woman. She's the first pear."

"What?"

"Arny Hayes was the second pear."

"Some broad was paying him off to get stories in the paper?"

"That's what it looks like."

"What kind of stories?"

"That's the part I can't figure out."

The phone rang. Ironhead glared at me for a few more moments and then answered it. "Hello?" Sounded downright unfriendly. That's a kind of characteristic reporter's reaction to all phone calls. You know some screwball is likely to be on the other end.

"Who?" said Ironhead. "Yeah, yeah . . ."

I had this feeling the phone call was about me, because Ironhead started watching me as he listened. He sort of groaned out a painful, "What?" And then another unhappy, "What?" Finally, he hung up the phone and looked at me a long time.

"You know who that was?"

I said hopefully. "Some screwball?"

"That was Detective Henderson."

"Oh, yeah—Steadman."

"Not Steadman—Henderson! He told me you gave some broad up on the West Side a hundred bucks that was police evidence."

"Oh yeah. Jeez." I hit myself on the side of the head. "Leeta."

"You told me a minute ago that you gave that five hundred to Marcia Pearl!" He was looking at me sideways as though there was a crick in his neck.

"Well . . . she needed it."

Ironhead grabbed up the phone. "Danny! Get me Dubbs!" He stared at me. "Dubbs? Listen, I want you to get up to . . . what's this Leeta's address?"

I told him.

". . . up to 210 West 56th Street and talk to Leeta Kane. Find out what she knows about Sandy Pearl. Find out why he was giving her bread. Get going." He hung up.

It was my turn to groan. "You know Dubbs is liable to spill this all into the paper, Ironhead," I said. "He's really nosy."

Well, I guess I ought to take one of those courses about How to Talk to the Boss, because Ironhead started yelling something more or less unintelligible and stomping around. He was the city editor, and he would take care of Dubbs and what the goddam hell was I talking about! Why was I trying to put him into a straitjacket and what was he supposed to tell the M.E.—not to mention the publisher—and I was absolutely not to step foot outside the office again—they would put a goddam cot for me in the sports department!—and didn't I know that Assistant District Attorney Eddie Kirkman was after me with a subpoena!

"Listen, Ironhead, I might as well tell you. They already served me with a subpoena."

His head popped forward again. He didn't say anything. I took the subpoena out of my jacket pocket and put it in front of him on the desk. He looked at it and then picked it up like it was something a skunk had piddled on.

He picked up the phone with a tired sigh. "Danny. Get me Corcoran." He hung up the phone. "Ten A.M. Thursday."

"They always say, 'in the forenoon.' "

"Is that what they always say?"

116

I decided to be quiet.

"You know what day this is?" Ironhead pointed to this calendar on the wall from Costello's bar. "Tuesday. That means this load of shit has to be crystal clear by Wednesday night. Because when you go to see that A.D.A. next Thursday morning, we've got to know everything there is to know!"

"How can I find out anything sleeping in the sports department?"

"You're not going to be in the sports department. You're not going to be in the office at all. I don't want to see your dopey puss. I don't want to hear any more of your goofy explanations. I want you to get the hell out there and find out who was paying off Sandy Pearl! And I want it all in a memo! A complete, logical, easily-understood memo!"

"Right."

"And when you have it all put together, you will feed everything to Dubbs Brewer, and he will write a story for Thursday's paper down to the last comma."

"Dubbs will write it?"

"Yes."

"I could do it."

"You, you dopey bastard, are one of what they like to call the dramatis personae. You can't write it."

I was almost out the door when I remembered something.

"Oh, listen, some of my contacts at State Supreme Court want Golden Gloves tickets."

Ironhead glared at me. "How many?"

"Well—ten."

His eyes widened. "Ten? Who goes?"

"Everybody."

"All right, goddammit. See Chuckie."

"Thanks." I started to go again. I looked back. "Oh, I almost forgot something else. You got any opera tickets?"

"What?"

"You know—the Met?"

"Goodbye!"

I left.

Chuckie the Nut Call Editor grumbled about the Golden Gloves tickets but handed them over. "All your cheapskate relatives." Like they were his own personal property, for Chris' sake.

I strolled over to the feature department to Kelly and Merola, who write this chichi celebrity page about all the phonies and freeloaders and party-goers in town and how they all goose each other over champagne at the St. Regis or something.

"Hey, Kelly," I said. "I need some Met tickets."

"Try sports," said Kelly, who was blipping away like a maniac on his Video Display Terminal, the electronic word processor that has replaced typewriters in newspaper offices.

"Naw, naw, not Mets—the Met. Opera tickets."

Kelly turned and looked up, as though noticing me for the first time.

"Opera tickets? *You* want opera tickets?"

"Luciano Pavarotti if you can."

"Hey, Merola, look who wants to go to the opera."

Well, after a certain amount of crap, Kelly called some press agent and said he'd have the opera tickets sent to me at the courthouse.

"Did Sandy Pearl ever ask you for free tickets?"

Kelly looked blank, which was his usual expression if you ask me, and said no.

I walked back to my desk and that window in the slot machine was in front of me again. There were the whirring wheels of pears, plums and bells. Sandy Pearl was going to pay for those opera tickets himself? Sandy Pearl had fishhooks in his pockets, but he was going to buy opera tickets for Al Wagner. One bell.

118

Wagner was watching the Amster Case for Sandy Pearl at Surrogate's Court. Two bells.

Sandy Fishhooks had a story he cared about enough to spend money to get it, but he wasn't writing about it. A plum.

I felt like calling up the State Casino Commission to complain.

18.

I remember one time in Dr. Holtzman the dentist's office I read a National Geographic magazine article about the Great Pyramid in Egypt. All these archaeologists were aglow with admiration over the way the ancient builders had fitted together 50-ton slabs of limestone without mortar, but with such perfection that you couldn't slide a knife blade between the blocks. I was beginning to think an Egyptian had built the Sandy Pearl case. I couldn't find an opening anywhere, either. Was it possible that there was no opening? Was it possible that Sandy Pearl wasn't being paid off and had really been knocked off by a hit-and-run car? Was the Sheldon Amster estate perfectly legitimate?

I picked up the phone and got Peggy the Operator.

"Fitzgerald, here. I want to call the Dutch Reformed Church out in Topeka, Kansas."

After Topeka information got the number for us, Peggy called the church and the Reverend Martin Schuyler came on the line.

"Hello?"

"Reverend Schuyler, this is Ed Fitzgerald at the New York *Daily Tribune*."

"Where?"

"New York. Reverend, I'm trying to get some information about a Maria Amster. She's one of your flock."

"My what?"

"She goes to your church."

"Maria Amster?"

"She got an affidavit from you about the Sheldon Amster estate."

"Oh, Mrs. Taylor."

"I thought her name was Amster."

"Yes, yes. It was. Her married name's Taylor. But I think she's divorced, so I guess she's an Amster again."

"Well, anyway, Reverend Schuyler, you signed an affidavit that her great-grandfather was a W.B. Amster?"

"Yes. It was just a technicality, I understand."

"Who told you that?"

"The lawyer. Just to get the estate settled. The church was left some money, and they needed this affidavit to get the estate settled."

"The Amster estate left your church some money?"

"Yes."

"How much?"

The pastor took a swallow of air and hesitated. "Who did you say this was?"

"Fitzgerald. *Daily Tribune.*"

"Why do you want this information?"

"Well, Reverend, I may be doing a story about the estate."

"Oh. Is it about to be settled? Can I tell the congregation the money will be released soon?"

"Well, it's not settled just yet, Reverend. How much was the church left?"

"Five hundred thousand dollars, I believe."

Don't you love it when people toss off some mind-boggling figure and then say, "I believe"? You don't forget a figure like that. All those Surrogate's Court papers fluttered through my head. I had seen no such paper. I had seen no bequests at all. But there were two feet of papers and I hadn't read all of them by any means. Still, it was interesting indeed that Sheldon Amster, who had died a bachelor in 1921 without a will, had left half a million dollars to a Kansas church.

"When did all this happen, Reverend?"

"Well, now, let me see. Mrs. Taylor came around to see

me about the time of her divorce. So that was about three years ago."

"The estate left money to your church three years ago?"

"Something like that. Yes. The lawyer called her about it, and she came in to see me."

"What lawyer called her?"

"From New York."

"Bernard Weinberg?"

"Yes, that's right. He had been trying to trace an heir for years, I understand, and finally he found Maria."

I'll say he had. And in Kansas, too.

"How did he happen to call her, do you know, Reverend?"

"Well, I think she had called him. After she saw the ad."

"What ad?"

"He ran an ad in the Topeka *Capital-Journal*, you know, trying to find any Amsters out here. And she answered. He was out here for a couple of weeks, digging into the church records. They walked around the graveyard, too."

"And they finally found that Maria was William Amster's great-granddaughter?"

"Oh, they knew that. It was whether W.B. Amster and William were the same person that was the technicality. Everybody out here always thought her great-grandfather came from New Orleans. But they finally got it straightened out."

"How?"

"Well, a judge certified it."

"What judge?"

"Back in New York."

"Reverend, I thought you were the one who certified that W.B. and William were the same man?"

"Well, no. Yes, I did. Yes and no. You see, it's one of those legal things. All I did was to certify that William Amster was buried here and that he was Mrs. Taylor's great-

122

grandfather. She certified that he was W.B. Amster, and I signed a paper that to the best of my knowledge he could be. Then it was up to that judge to accept it or not, and I guess he did."

Lovely. The reverend says it's up to the judge, and the judge says if it's all right with the reverend, it's all right with him.

There was one more intriguing loose end.

"Reverend Schuyler, did you say the estate left the church money? Or was it Mrs. Amster?"

"You mean Mrs. Taylor?"

"Yes, Maria."

"Well, it's six of one and half a dozen of the other, isn't it?"

"Not exactly, pastor."

"The lawyer . . ."

"Weinberg?"

". . . Mr. Weinberg . . . explained to me that an estate can make any bequests necessary to get itself settled, and Mrs. Taylor said she knew her great-grandfather would want this done."

"I see."

And I did see, finally. It was beautiful. A little for the church, a little for Maria, a little for the lawyer. That's the way lawyers do business, isn't it? They're scavengers who tidy up the leavings of the rich who litter up the courts with forgotten millions.

"Can you describe Maria, Reverend?"

"Well . . ." He took a breath. "I don't know. About average height. Very pretty woman, you know."

"Pretty?"

"Yes, yes. More than pretty."

"Beautiful?"

"You could say that. But very religious. We're getting a new altar, you know."

"Have you got any pictures of her?"

"Pictures? Why, no. Is anything wrong?"

"Oh, no. It's just an interesting story. Maria is a beautiful blonde with a faint accent, isn't she?"

"She doesn't have any accent that I know of. You people in New York have got the accents." He laughed in that Midwest manner.

"Do you know where she is?"

"Why, I think she's in New York."

"Any idea where?"

"Why don't you call that lawyer? He should know."

That would be Weinberg. Yes, I certainly would have to ask old parchment face a few questions.

"Or you might ask Roscoe Schaaf," the pastor said, somewhat hesitantly.

"Who?"

"He's a friend of hers. Since the divorce. She and Sam Taylor got divorced, you know."

"Where would I find Schaaf?"

"Well, he's in the book here."

"Thanks."

"Say, can you let me know when things are settled? We're all very excited, you know."

"Sure, Reverend."

I hung up the phone and had Peggy get Roscoe Schaaf's number from information in Topeka. I called, but there was no answer.

I wasn't too unhappy about that, though. Because finally I had something concrete to pursue. A contradiction. If Reverend Schuyler would swear that his church had been promised $500,000 from the estate and there was no such bequest, it would be a knife blade in between all those perfectly fitted slabs. All I needed was one more crack at those court papers, and I could go to Eddie Kirkman, the assistant D.A., who was after me. If I could lay something solid

124

on him, he might overlook the fact that the information came from sealed court papers.

Clickety-clickety-clickety back down the F.D.R. Drive to the courthouse again. I hurried to the probate clerk's office and was confronted by a stout little woman at a typewriter.

"Is Al Wagner around?" She looked at me in some alarm and stood up. "Are you that reporter who keeps calling?"

"Yes."

The woman was halfway across the room toward a door to an inner office. "Mr. Davis!"

A man stepped out from the inner office.

"That's the reporter who keeps calling."

"What's the matter?" I asked Davis.

He walked over to me. Large with a gray suit and a red striped shirt. "Lester Davis. I'm the probate clerk here. Has Wagner been showing you sealed court papers?"

I felt like a kid in school again facing a stern principal who already knew everything. "Sealed papers?"

"Wagner has been reprimanded and reassigned."

Davis turned and walked away. Lt. Dickson could not have frozen me out more emphatically.

But I was too close to a solution now. I went back out into the corridor, down the back way to the frosted door that led to the file room. I slipped in quietly and let the door close behind me. When I slid open the filing cabinet where Wagner had put the Amster estate papers, the drawer was empty.

19.

THE reason you can't get to the bottom of things is because the bottom keeps shifting like a sunken battleship moving beneath you. There I was trying to get a line on Maria Amster and Al Wagner is yanked from beneath me. All I needed was one more look at those papers, and suddenly they were no longer available. Somebody was still one step ahead of me.

And then it occurred to me that, with the Amster Case about to be heard in court, the judge might have taken the papers to look them over. Wagner had said the case was assigned to Judge Foley.

That rang a bell. Judge Herbert Foley, the dapper surrogate I had seen lunching with Weinberg at Giambone's. I rode the elevator up into the gloomy higher reaches of the old museum, and finally found my way to the court officer who guarded the way to the inner sanctum, and past him to the judge's secretary. After the court clerk and the secretary looked me over suspiciously, I was shown into the judge's office. It was like being in some floating tower in a Hapsburg palace in old Vienna.

"Hello, Judge. I'm Ed Fitzgerald, *Daily Tribune*."

"Yes, yes, of course. How are you?" Judges are like that. They always smile and treat you like a lifelong friend, even if they haven't the faintest idea of who you are. They do, that is, if you're from a newspaper.

"Judge, I'm trying to find out about an estate case that I think is about to come up before you. The Sheldon Amster estate."

Judge Foley frowned, as though trying to recall the case, and then he looked at the floor. "Amster?" he said. "Is it on the calendar?'' He shuffled some papers on his desk and then smiled at me. ''Uh, I'm not sure if a firm date has been set on that.''

''I thought it was on for Thursday.''

''Who told you that?'' The judge smiled, and I realized I only knew about it because Al Wagner had gotten it from sealed papers.

''Somebody told me, Judge.''

It all seemed to be of the least possible concern to him. Just another case in an endless calendar of estates. ''Can you give me any details of it?''

''No, not really.''

Judge Foley looked at more papers and then suddenly he smiled. ''Oh, I think that case has been sealed by request of the parties. Yes, it's sealed.'' He smiled pleasantly, as though that solved everything.

''Do you have the papers, Judge?''

Pink face and clear eyes as impassive as the walls of a great granite citadel. Could I possibly be asking him additional questions? ''That case is sealed,'' he repeated, a trifle more pointedly. Sealed papers. Judicial impregnability.

''Your honor, I really need to get a look at those papers.''

The judge seemed to focus on my face for the first time. ''Are you the reporter that was bothering one of our clerks?''

''I wasn't 'bothering' him. Just asking about the Amster estate.''

''The probate clerk was up here, very upset.''

''Judge Foley, the papers have disappeared. I was trying to examine them, and . . .''

''You were trying to examine sealed papers?''

''They're the answer to the whole thing. Somebody must have known I was going to look into them, and they stole the papers.''

''I'm sure the papers are not 'stolen,' young man,'' the

judge said, becoming rigid. "The lawyer no doubt has them."

Weinberg had them? Of course.

"Judge, this is Bernard Weinberg's case. It's an estate involving a Maria Amster."

"Mr. Fitzgerald, I believe I told you this is a private matter. It's settled, also, I believe."

"Settled?"

"Virtually. If you wish to find out anything about the matter, you should contact Mr. Weinberg. It would be up to him and his client. They requested that the papers be sealed."

"How can I get them unsealed?"

"What standing do you have?"

"Standing?"

He gave me a lengthy, judicial sigh. "Do you have any legal interest in this estate?"

"No. Not directly. You see . . ."

"I'm sorry."

I looked at him, staring as hard as I could into those impassive fluid eyes. I was running into a barrier again. The judge's alert eyes blinked and he seemed to be watching me with the scrutiny of a sentry.

"It's really up to the lawyer," he finally said. Judge Foley was not the one to talk to. His hands were tied. He was an innocent party, he seemed to be suggesting.

"You can't help me at all, Judge?" I tried to imply that he was being given a last chance to speak out. If he had anything to say.

"I'm afraid not." The sentry eyes were gone, and only the kindliness of a disinterested jurist stared out at me.

"Okay, your honor," I said. "Thanks." I tried to make it sound properly ominous, like the marshal of Dodge City giving Cole Younger one last chance to talk before it came to six-shooters on the dusty street.

The judge seemed no longer interested.

Back toward State Supreme Court in an absolute funk. What the hell had I stumbled upon? Had Sandy Pearl had any idea of what he was up against? The impossible conclusion hammering away inside my head was that the judge had to be in on it, too, whatever it was.

Another of those hideous "good news and bad news" situations raced through my mind. "The good news is that now I know a lawyer and a judge are behind this and they've sealed the papers. The bad news is there's no way to find out what the hell they've done."

20.

WHEN I walked into my little press room, there sat Tweedledum and Tweedledee, smiling and looking satisfied with themselves.

Big Dan Langner took his usual legs apart stance, probably the same stance he used when he had a jump ball for Bishop Malloy, and made his official announcement.

"Well, it's all wrapped up."

"What?"

Marty Stevens took out his little notebook and flipped open the pages.

"We've located him," said Langner.

"Who?"

"Tony Faso."

Marty Stevens glanced at his notebook. "Denver, Colorado," he said, and flipped his book shut.

"We're flying out to get him."

"What do you want him for?"

Big smirk from Stevens. Disdainful glance from Langner.

"That's the case," said Langner. "Tony Faso knocked off his ex-wife because she was bugging him about alimony payments, see?"

Stevens's book flapped open again. "He was all over Fordham Road the night before she was murdered lapping it up." He wet his fingertip and put it on the notebook. "Perpetrator told witness he was fed up with being bled white by victim." He looked up. "That's a quote." Flap shut.

"Tony Faso couldn't have killed Rita."

"Why not?"

"Because, dammit," I spluttered, "Rita was killed by the same gun that killed Arny Hayes."

"So?"

"Couldn't have been Tony."

"Why not?"

"I thought you said Arny got it from loan sharks?"

"Sure," said Langner. "Tony Faso must have been working for the sharks."

They had a foolproof, wonderful system. The case was a huge vat of tar and everything they found they just dumped in and kept stirring until it all blended together.

"It just doesn't add up," I mumbled.

The Stevens notebook flapped open. Wet the finger. Traced down the scribbled notes. "Suspect admits he went to victim's apartment on night of the murder. Suspect states he 'wiped up the floor' with ex-wife. Unquote."

Langner smiled. "When he read in the paper that she was dead, he beats it to Colorado."

"He admits he shot her?"

"He does."

"Have they got the gun?"

"The weapon has not been recovered." Stevens got that from his notebook.

"How bombed was he that night?"

"He'd had a few."

"Does he remember what really happened?"

"He does now."

They turned to go.

"Look, Langner, if you want to do something worthwhile, how about stopping off in Topeka, Kansas, and finding out who Maria Amster is."

"Who?"

"She's the beneficiary of a big estate in Surrogate's Court. See, Sandy Pearl was digging into that case when he got knocked off."

131

"The Sanford Pearl case isn't murder."

"Aw, Jesus god! I'm telling you, every time I dig further into the case somebody drops dead."

"Nobody's going to drop dead anymore, Fitzgerald," smiled Langner. "Not as long as Tony Faso is in the can in Denver."

So, there it was. As far as I was concerned, it had nothing to do with Tony Faso. As far as they were concerned, it had everything to do with him.

"Why don't you stick to writing stories?" said Stevens. "You guys always want to make every two-bit homicide a TV series."

With that snappy remark they walked out, headed for Denver, no doubt.

I put in another call to Roscoe Schaaf in Topeka, Kansas, but there was still no answer. It was wonderful. Maria Amster was in New York City somewhere, right under my nose, and I couldn't find her. Roscoe Schaaf might be able to tell me where she was, but he was lost somewhere in the Kansas wheatfields. Al Wagner had vanished. Tony Faso was in Denver. I was desperate to find somebody—anybody—but afraid to go looking for them.

21.

"EVER hear of the Sheldon Amster estate?" I asked Reeves when he stuck his head in the door the next morning.

"What?"

"The Sheldon Amster case. Sandy Pearl was chasing it."

Reeves stood on one foot and then on the other and wagged his head like a lion that has to pee. "Aw, Jesus," he said. "Sheldon Amster? Yeah, sure. It was a big story years ago."

"It's Weinberg's."

"So?"

"Nothing. Has he mentioned it to you?"

"Naw. It's old stuff."

"He hasn't been after you to write about it?"

"What's to write? It must have been dropped or settled years ago."

"No, it hasn't been. It's coming up tomorrow."

"Listen, let me give you a tip. You write a story out of Surrogate's Court, the desk will be on your ass to cover it all the time. We don't want to be responsible for any of those damned wills."

"Nobody really covers that court?"

"Not much. Once in a while. It's way down by City Hall, for Chris' sake. Listen, you want to find out about the damned thing? I'm having lunch with Weinberg. I'll ask him."

"No, no," I said. "I'll probably be over."

"Is that so?" said Reeves. "Well, well, it's Boy Scout day again, is it? Listen, Plonker, there's one condition. You're not to act like a swine, as you usually do."

"Up yours."

It was time—past time—to talk to Weinberg about the case. I think I was hesitant because I was afraid he would be able to explain everything away, and it would be back to square one again. And it didn't seem to me that there were any more square ones left.

When I got to Giambone's, I found Weinberg was the guest of honor at a going-away lunch.

"You going to pinch a few fannies on the Via Veneto?" Reeves challenged Weinberg.

"I'm afraid my interest will be more statuary," he said and smiled.

"You're going away?" I asked.

"We're stuck here checking on pothole suits, and the traveler's heading for Rome," said Reeves. "A city I helped save for the *Italianos* from the dirty Nazis, by the way." He smiled in recollection. "Listen, look up a joint called Taverna Margutta."

"You're going to Rome, Counselor?"

"Yes," said Weinberg. "My first trip to Europe."

"Anywhere else?"

"Holland. And maybe Paris."

It sounded like a getaway, all of a sudden.

"Does this mean you're retiring?" I asked with what I hoped was an innocent expression. Weinberg's eyes darted to my face alertly, but the glacier did not crack.

"Aw, what are you babbling about?" said Reeves. "Retire? Him? He'll be drumming up business in his coffin."

But Weinberg never did deny it. Going to Holland, was he? Maybe to do a little more business on the Amster estate? My circumstantial house of cards was turning into a sprawling castle in Holland and Rome. I was trying to decide how to approach him when Reeves did it for me.

"What's all this crap about the Amster Case?" he blurted out.

I glanced at Weinberg, but his face remained fixed in that placid smile.

"What case?" asked Weinberg. "Sheldon Amster?"

"Fitzboggen just discovered it. Forty years late," said Reeves, and strolled over to listen to a story Judge Nacht was orchestrating at the next table.

I looked at Weinberg. Not a sign of alarm or concern or hint of guilt.

"Interesting case," I ventured.

"Fairly routine," said Frozen Face.

"I'm thinking about writing a piece on it," I said casually. Maybe that would crack that glacier.

"Not much to it." The granite ice shelf was as before.

"Why don't you fill me in, Counselor?"

"Well, I'd love to, Fitzgerald, but the papers have been sealed."

"Couldn't you just give the outline?"

He laughed easily. "I'm afraid that's impossible. The Association of the Bar of the City of New York would not be pleased." Weinberg sipped some tonic water. "Besides, my client doesn't want any publicity."

Was there the tiniest pinpoint glint of malice deep in the pupils of Weinberg's eyes behind his rimless glasses? If so, it disappeared in his smile. A perverse sort of pleasure went through me as he sat there denying the importance of the Amster Case. Finally the electrical current seemed to be making some kind of contact. I had hit another barrier.

"I'm afraid it's quite ordinary."

"Well, Counselor," I said, "I'll be in court bright and early tomorrow morning to find out."

Weinberg looked at me. "Tomorrow?"

"It's on the calendar for tomorrow morning, right?"

"Why, no," said Weinberg.

"I think I saw it listed in the *Law Journal*."

Weinberg laughed again. "Oh yes, you're right. It was on

for tomorrow, but there's been another adjournment. It's rescheduled for—let me see—two weeks, I think. The twenty-sixth."

"What?"

"It's that kind of case, Fitzgerald. Drags on and on. It may never get settled."

"Didn't Amster die without a will?"

"I'm really sorry, Fitzgerald, but I can't go into that."

"Where did Maria Amster come from?"

The glint reappeared, deep in the pupils, burning brightly for a passing moment. Then he laughed.

"I wish I could satisfy your evident curiosity, Fitzgerald. But I'm under the strictures of a rigid profession."

I hadn't meant to challenge Weinberg head-on like that, but I was getting edgy. We were heading for some kind of a showdown, that was certain. I had to find my way out of the damned legal thicket.

"Maybe I *can* satisfy your curiosity," said Weinberg, smiling pleasantly. "You see, it's a matter of some delicacy. It's for a friend. I'm not getting anything out of it."

"A friend?"

"A lovely one. It involves a few thousand dollars, at most."

Weinberg smiled a vulnerable smile, as though confessing he was only a man with human weaknesses. A surge of bitter disgust went through me as I realized the "friend" was Belinda Sharpe, the lovely blonde for whom I had felt sorry. So that was what she saw in him.

"What's the fee, Counselor?" I asked flatly, as though needing to know the worst.

Weinberg only smiled.

What difference did it make? Belinda was nothing to me. Only a somewhat adrift victim who had discovered a way to solve her problems by pandering to his.

"I have several other cases of considerably more inter-

136

est," Weinberg was saying. "Why don't you let me fill you in on one of them?"

"I'm only interested in the Amster Case."

"I have another case. It concerns a negligence suit. It would be far more rewarding."

"Rewarding?"

"Journalistically." He smiled. "And otherwise, if one were interested."

I glared at him. Was this a bribe offer?

"I've heard tell that reporters have been known to get, say, five hundred dollars for becoming interested," I said.

Weinberg paled a little and his lips compressed. "I have heard that, too."

"I've also heard that people who got too interested ended up dead."

Weinberg chuckled, "Now, really."

"Yes, really."

Do you know what it's like to look into a smiling face that is pulsating with a hatred that seems to radiate outward like an electric heater?

22.

"WELL, you disappeared before the tab arrived, I see."
Reeves stood in my doorway weaving back and forth. "As
usual," he chirped. "What the hell did you say to Weinberg?"

"Why?"

"He got up and left like he was double-parked."

"Listen, Harry, how do you go after a judge?"

"What?"

"Let's say a smart lawyer is pulling a fast one on a case
and he's got a judge in on it with him to seal the papers.
How do I write about that?"

"I'll tell you how," said Reeves. "You write about it and
then they drive a truck up to the back door of the *Trib* and
cart the presses away. What are you talking about?"

I sighed. "What do you know about Judge Foley?"

"The surrogate?"

"Yeah. Are Judge Foley and Weinberg an item?"

"You're too much, Fitzbog, you know that?"

"How about broads? Either of them into broads?"

"Aw, for Chris' sake." Reeves's ruddy face shook in annoyance. "Weinberg's a widower. Was married for around
forty years to one woman."

"How about Foley?"

"You've seen him in Giambone's. A good roll in the hay
would put him in Queen of Heaven Cemetery, for god's
sake."

"The damned Amster Case is what this is all about and
they've sealed it."

"Aw, what do you mean? It's been around for forty
years."

"I'm telling you, they're pulling off an underground burglary. It's like a damned basement Brink's job in broad daylight."

"A judge and a big lawyer? Why would they do that?"

"I don't know. They're both along in years. Maybe they want to retire to Rome."

Reeves revolved his head with annoyed disbelief. "Aw, Jesus."

"Well, why not? If they hooked up together, they could swipe it easily."

"It would have to be plenty of loot. It isn't that big. How much is in the damned estate?"

"I don't know. Over a million."

"That's supposed to be big bucks? A million, for Chris' sake?"

"It could be more, couldn't it? They're giving half a million to a church."

Reeves smiled and nodded his head at the wisdom of my suspicions. "A million and they're giving half to a church and you've got a Brink's job, huh? You'll get a merit badge for this one, all right. All you have to do is bag a lawyer, a judge and a church." I could hear him chortling all the way back across the lobby as he toddled to his press room.

The slot machine was before me again, the wheels whirring. Errrrra-thump. A judge. Errrrrrra-thump. A lawyer. Errrrrrrra-thump. A minister. Then the jackpot rushed over me—endless abuse from Ironhead, three libel suits, ostracism and maybe a job on some weekly in Cape May, New Jersey. But it wouldn't leave me alone. Those burning eyes in Giambone's transfixed me. I was in too deep now. I got on the phone.

"Marv, I'm still trying to get a line on that Amster thing."

Marvin exhaled with annoyance. "I can't read all that stuff to you."

"I know, Marv. I'm just looking for the value of the estate."

"I don't see anything here," said Marvin. "Just says it's supposed to be over a million bucks."

Over a million. A lot of money, all right. But Reeves was right. When you considered that the church was supposed to get half a million, and there were lawyers' fees and court costs, there wouldn't be all that much left.

"Do the most recent stories quote anybody?"

Papers rustled over the phone. Marv said, "An assistant state attorney general—James Pritchett."

"Pritchett. Okay. What year is that clip?"

"Looks like 1948, Fitz."

A call to the state attorney general's office, but Pritchett had retired years ago. It took another call out to Nassau County to find his son, who told me his father was now feeding pelicans on Long Key in the Florida Keys.

"Hello, Peggy? It's Fitzgerald. I have to call Long Key in Florida."

"Business?"

"Yes, Peggy."

Before the call went through, Morty Owens, the assistant city editor under Ironhead, came on the line.

"Hey, Fitz," he said. "What are all these long-distance calls? Ironhead's getting on my butt."

"Owney, I've got to find this broad who's getting a big payoff in an estate."

"Yeah? Where is she?"

"Right here in New York someplace."

"So why are you calling Kansas?"

"I'm not. She's not there. I'm calling the Florida Keys."

"You said she's here in town."

"She is. But I got to find the guy who handled this case back in 1948."

Owney went silent for a minute. "Fitz, Ironhead told me

to find out what the hell you're doing because he can't make any sense out of you. I can't either."

"Trust me, Owney."

"What do I tell Ironhead?"

"Tell him I owe him a kiss."

"Thanks, Fitz. This better make sense sooner or later."

Finally I got the retired James Pritchett on the phone from Long Key. "What case?" he said in a surprisingly lively voice. "Amster?" I could imagine him shaking his head in recollection. "I remember it well. What a headache."

"Well, Mr. Pritchett, what I'm trying to figure out is what the total value of the estate was."

He chuckled. "There was a lot of palaver about that, I'll tell you. We finally fixed it at two hundred and forty million dollars."

I went blank for a moment.

"Of course, that was some years ago," he said. "It's probably a lot more now if it's still unsettled."

23.

You know how it is when you sit up in the middle of the night and suddenly know what that elusive word in the *Times* Sunday crossword puzzle is? All of a sudden, I had the whole thing. Weinberg telling me the Amster estate was a few thousand dollars at most and that he was just doing it for a friend clinched it for me.

Weinberg and Judge Foley were looting the Amster estate of $240 million, which certainly made it worth a lot of trouble. One pear.

Belinda Sharpe was really Maria Amster. Two pears. She had delivered those envelopes to Sandy Pearl. So she's not brunette. She wore a wig. She dyed her hair. Belinda was helping Weinberg and the judge steal the Amster estate. Three pears.

All I needed to know was when the case would be on Judge Foley's calendar in Surrogate's Court. That would be the one time they would all have to surface together for at least long enough to officially declare the case settled and to have it entered into the court record.

Al Wagner had said it was on for tomorrow, and Weinberg told me it had been postponed until the twenty-sixth. With Judge Foley controlling the court, they could postpone or reschedule the case for any time they liked.

I would have to try to protect myself as best I could. I called the photo assignment desk.

"Hey, Pete. Fitzgerald."

"Dull day, Fitz. Why don't you find us a stiff?"

"Thanks, Pete. I needed that. Listen, I'm going to need a photog at Manhattan Surrogate's Court tomorrow morning."

"What time?"

"About nine, nine-thirty. It's in Judge Herbert Foley's courtroom, and it's titled the Sheldon Amster Estate."

"Okay."

"Tell the photog to get a shot of Maria Amster."

"Who's she?"

"She's the one who's getting all the bread."

"Is she a good-looking broad?"

"Is the Pope Catholic? A terrific-looking blonde."

All of a sudden Ironhead came on the line, demanding to know where the hell I disappear to all the time.

"I've been at Surrogate's Court."

"I thought you didn't want to cover Surrogate's Court?"

"I don't. But I think Judge Foley is in on it."

"Who?"

"Judge Foley, the Manhattan surrogate, is in on this, too."

There was a loud silence. That's the only way I can describe it. Ironhead said nothing, but I could hear him anyway, sort of gasping or choking.

"Fitz, you aren't going after a judge, too? Is it your mission in life to drive the *Daily Tribune* to destruction?"

"Ironhead, he's got to be in on it. Weinberg couldn't pull this off unless the judge sealed those papers."

"In on what?"

"Some hanky-panky about an estate in Surrogate's Court. I think Sandy was onto them."

That seemed to please Ironhead immensely. "He was going to break the story and they knocked him off?"

"That's what it looks like. But I wonder why that woman was paying him off."

"You mean Rita who got killed?"

"No. It must have been Maria."

Another strangled silence. "Who's Maria?"

143

"She's the one who's getting the estate. It's all becoming clear."

"To who? Keep in touch. Don't fall into any goddam sewer this time. And don't go after any judge without talking to me and Corcoran."

I wasn't going after any judge. Or after Weinberg, either. I had stirred things up enough that I couldn't hang around them.

They couldn't settle the case without the presence of Maria Amster. I decided that Maria/Belinda and I were going to be inseparable from now on.

24.

UNLIKE the elusive Rita, Belinda wasn't hard to find. She had been hanging around the various courts of Foley Square like a groupie. I realized, of course, that it was all because she was sticking close to Weinberg, and probably shadowing me. I know it doesn't make sense, but I got angry every time I thought of Weinberg and Belinda together. How much was Belinda giving old parchment face? It isn't smart to care for somebody you're trying to catch.

I spotted her getting out of the elevator in my courthouse. She walked across the great rotunda, and even smiled when she saw me. She headed right to me.

"I've been sitting in on a trial," she beamed. "Fascinating."

"It is, sometimes," I said. What I wanted to do was to walk her past the booth of John the information clerk so he could get a look at her. I was confident that John would be able to identify her as the woman who brought Sandy Pearl those envelopes, even if her hair was now blonde.

"Have you ever seen my office?" I asked, like a spider to a fly.

"I walked by and looked in, but you weren't there." Then she blushed at the admission.

"Come on."

I walked her by John's booth, but of course he was gone. Out getting down his horse bets, probably.

I made a feeble pretense of "showing" her my office, but how do you show off a gloomy cubicle with a battered desk and some old metal lockers? Still, Belinda looked around with lively interest, her intelligent eyes darting about to examine everything. She had a fetching quality of seeming to be totally interested in whatever was shown to her. It annoyed me all over again to think that she had been taken in by Weinberg.

After a few minutes, there was no way to continue stalling in my cubby hole, so I left a note in John's booth inviting him to join me at lunch at Brady's over on Broadway.

Belinda and I strolled across Foley Square and over to Broadway to Brady's, where I knew almost no one and thought we would not be spotted together. It was a place John often went after making his OTB bets. I'll say this for Belinda/Maria—she was the coolest conspirator you could possibly imagine. She walked along smiling and chatting and having a good time.

"You seem changed," I said when we were in a booth.

"I am. For the first time in a long time, I feel . . . free."

Free—as in independently wealthy?

"Why is that?"

"Well, I'm out of a claustrophobic marriage. I'm getting myself launched into a new life. I was afraid, I admit it. But now . . ."

Vitality was what I saw in the lively face and manner of Belinda. Bright, alert, lovely blue eyes and an inviting yet independent style.

John wasn't in Brady's, of course. He was seldom available when you wanted him. We had Reuben sandwiches and talked some more, as I watched the door for John.

"What happened to the marriage?"

"Thomas—my former husband—somehow missed his target, and I'm afraid we were both casualties. He couldn't handle the disappointment, I guess."

"What was he trying to do?"

"Thomas is a teacher. He needed a certain position. He didn't think it suitable that I should be a lawyer, for instance."

"You're a lawyer?"

"Yes. But I've never really practiced. Thomas thought it wouldn't look right. So, I stayed home and read and grew a little garden. After a while, I was afraid to do much of anything."

A lawyer? Well, well, well. So Belinda was not the poor, unknowing victim after all. She knew what she was doing! My brain reeled. But she was seemingly unaware, and went right on chatting.

Thomas, her pompous teacher of a former husband, had more or less smothered her, said Belinda, until she lost her confidence. And when he was passed over for promotion to a full professorship and department head at Queens College, Thomas resigned and announced he was moving to Virginia to be headmaster at a private school for boys.

"It was clear he did not think I would fit in in Virginia," she said. "I had become too . . . reclusive . . . you see." She smiled.

"Do you have some sort of an accent?" I ventured.

She blushed again and then laughed. "My, you do have a good ear, Mr. Fitzgerald. And what do you suppose it is?"

"I don't know. Midwestern possibly?"

Well, the formerly reclusive Belinda Sharpe showed she could laugh when I said that. She virtually exploded with mirth and watched me in a wonderment of little giggly chirps.

"Heavens!" She laughed some more. "You must have some Welsh coal miners out there. Midwestern? My dear man, I was born in Wales!"

The accent certainly did sound faintly British, now that she had explained it.

"In fact, I even have some kind of a title in the genealogical mists," she said. "Actually, I could be addressed as Lady Wentworth." She laughed again. She was having a good time, and I'm afraid she had completely taken me in.

147

It was so hard to see this beautiful, vibrant woman in such a situation.

"So you got a divorce," I said, needing to bring it back into context. "Bernie Weinberg handled it?"

"Yes. Mr. Weinberg has been very helpful. I don't know what I would have done without him."

"Have you ever been to Kansas?"

Not a ripple in those clear eyes. "Kansas? No, I'd love to see it, though."

"How about Rome?"

"Ah, now you're in my territory. It's surely the most fascinating city in the world."

"Isn't it, though? I have a fantasy of eventually moving there and covering Rome for the paper."

"Really? When?"

"Oh, there's no 'when' to it. That's down the road, if it ever happens."

"You have to have a dream for it to come true, Ed."

How wonderful was Belinda in such moments. All full of encouragement, support, empathy. Her former husband Thomas had clearly been a fool. If, indeed, there really was a Thomas.

"Have you been to Rome recently?"

A faraway look, a sigh. "No. I've thought of going back."

"When?"

"I had thought of going very soon. But my plans are uncertain at the moment." She smiled ingenuously.

Well, my dear, all the uncertainty will be dissolved tomorrow in Surrogate's Court when Weinberg gets his hands on the money and you can both flit away to the Eternal City. Gloom slid through the bottom of my mind.

"Actually, I have my first case now, and I just might go into law after all," said Belinda. "A friend of mine—an artist—is about to be evicted from a loft, and I'm going to represent her in Landlord and Tenant Court."

"Is that so? When?"

"Tomorrow morning."

So Belinda/Maria was going to Landlord and Tenant Court tomorrow morning, was she? When the Amster Case was being settled in Surrogate's Court? More cat and mouse. But this time I was not to be misled. I had the quarry in my sight and I had no intention of letting it get away. The one fact I clung to was that the Amster estate could not be settled without the presence of Belinda. I would go where she went.

"Mind if I come along and watch you operate?" I suggested.

She took it as a compliment. "That's very sweet of you."

John the information booth clerk lived up to his reputation of never being in the booth when you needed information, or in Brady's when you needed him to identify someone.

I ended up driving Belinda out to Sunnyside, Queens, in my pumpkin Pinto. She had an apartment on a sidestreet off Queens Boulevard, up from the Queensborough Bridge. She didn't invite me in, as Rita had. But then Belinda was a different entity, and after all she didn't have to. But at the last minute before she went in she leaned over and gave me a little kiss and a dazzling smile, as though saying she was extremely happy that we had met. Then, with several light steps, she was gone.

I drove back over the bridge into Manhattan in a foul mood.

25.

I had the feeling that Belinda had set me up again, because as I walked to my apartment building the two hulking nameless ones got out of a car and stopped me.

"Hi," said Henderson. "Eddie Kirkman asked us to stop by and remind you of your appointment with him tomorrow at the D.A.'s office."

"Tomorrow?"

"You've got your subpoena, I hope?" said Henderson.

"I've got it."

"Ten A.M."

"Listen, I'd like to postpone that for a few days."

Henderson smiled. Steadman shook his head.

"You know what a subpoena means? It means now."

"But this whole thing is a mess. I haven't got any answers."

"We'll get all that straightened out, won't we?" said Steadman. "Kirkman is real good at asking questions and getting answers."

"Have you guys found out anything?"

"Oh, plenty," smiled Henderson.

"Like what?"

"Like you give away hundred-dollar bills that are evidence."

"Oh, that."

"Yes, that. Who gave you the hundred?"

"That's what I'd like to know."

Henderson looked at Steadman. "He doesn't know who gave him a hundred dollars, Steadman. Are there people giving you hundred-dollar bills that you can't remember?"

"Lots of people," said Steadman.

"Who?"

"Can't remember."

"Look, I explained all that in the memo—which you Sneaky Petes stole from me. I found the hundred in an envelope."

"Imagine!" said Henderson. "He finds money and gives it away to a strange woman."

"Easy come, easy go," said Steadman.

"Hey, Fitzgerald," said Henderson. "Did Tony Faso know you were balling his wife?"

"What?"

"Tony Faso."

"You mean Rita? They were divorced. I only met her one time."

"How many times you think it would take to get Tony upset?"

"What's all this about Tony Faso?"

An inhale by Henderson. That superior detective look that suggests you couldn't find the way to the john. Another look by Steadman that says he and Henderson share the same feeling. They look at each other. Then at me.

"You'd like to make this a big, elaborate deal. Well, how about a simple, straightforward deal? Tony Faso's a muscle man for the loan sharks. He does a little job for them on Arny Hayes. Then, Tony finds out some guy's banging his wife. He does a little job on her. Then, the guy who's been balling Tony's wife gets a little shook up. He cooks up a story to take the heat off himself."

I looked at them in amazement. It never ceases to astound me how many different explanations can come from the same set of facts. They were cooking up a case against me!

They walked away.

26.

I took no chances on Belinda/Maria giving me the slip the next morning. I was parked up from her Queens apartment at six-thirty. When she came out, I followed as she got a cab on Queens Boulevard and headed into Manhattan. I was sure she was heading for Surrogate's Court, but she got out at Landlord and Tenant Court. I parked behind Police Headquarters and hurried over to catch up with her.

I don't know if you've ever been in Landlord and Tenant Court, but it has to be something like what is meant by "bedlam." Reporters don't often use a word like cacophony to describe things, but it would fit the tumultuous noise that exists there. The racket is only the first thing that hits you. Next it's the jammed corridors and rooms, and then it's the confusion, and finally it's the feeling that nobody gives a good goddam. It's every man for himself, each tenant trying to get his or her problem solved, and each landlord trying to do the same.

Inside the tall, glass-walled front lobby people were milling around yelling and shoving and trying to find out where to go. I found Belinda and her client in the midst of it, swimming through the chaos like salmon going upstream. Terry Lamp, her client, was a wild-eyed thing wearing an expression of distrust and defiance. You had the feeling she didn't believe anything you or anyone else said.

Belinda stuck up a hand and waved at me briefly, but was unable to escape the nonstop harangue Terry Lamp was giving her about her Caligula of a landlord. Everyone around us seemed also to be shrieking and screaming at each other about endless wrongs. The uninterrupted howling continued until finally the doors of the court opened, and there was a mad crush and scramble inside. Everybody poured in, shouting that they had been there twice before—three times—four—a dozen!

"The plaster falls in the lasagna," a woman yelled.

"No rent until he fixes the pipes."

"My client cannot make repairs when no rent is paid!"

"Order! Please sit down until your name is called. If you can't find a seat, please go out. No one may stand." The court officer shoved his way through the yelling mob.

I pushed my way up to the front well of the court and found Sol Goldstein, the court clerk.

"Solly, can you tell me when a case is going to be on— Lamp versus Stern?"

Solly glanced at me nervously and his finger slid down a column on a long court calendar page, making swift little glides.

"Nope," he said, and went to the second page.

"Nope," he said, and went to the third.

His finger did little skids down the endless column and then suddenly stopped near the bottom of the third page. "Eviction action?"

"Yeah."

"It'll be a while," he said with a deep sigh.

I glanced at the page. More than a hundred cases were on the calendar call ahead of Belinda's client.

"It's going to take a while," I told Belinda. "I think I'll hop across to Manhattan Supreme Court and see if anything's doing."

"Okay," she smiled. "Thanks for stopping by." She squeezed my hand. An actress, was Belinda.

I slipped out into the corridor and into a phone booth from where I could watch the courtroom door. The situation was perfect, I reasoned. She could slip away out to Surrogate's Court, get the Amster estate settled, and get back to

Landlord and Tenant Court without being missed. When she went, I would follow.

I called Danny the switchboard guy at the *Daily Trib*, and he almost exploded into the phone.

"Boy, are you in trouble!"

"I know."

"Where are you? They're waiting for you at the D.A.'s office."

"Listen, Danny. Ask Ironhead if he can get me a postponement."

"I'm not asking Ironhead anything. *You* ask him. He said if you called to switch you over to him. He says they're going to hold you in contempt or something. Hold on . . ."

I hung up. I had no better answers for Ironhead than I had for the D.A. or Corcoran.

I stuck my head back into the courtroom, and stayed in the back watching Belinda and Terry Lamp. For once, I felt on top of things and safe from Ironhead and Kirkman, who would never find me here. Every so often Belinda would look around anxiously, and I was ready to follow her. But she always sat back down, or was tugged back down by her client. An hour went by. Two hours. Three. Belinda waited and so did I.

Finally, the calendar call ended and the harried judge began hearing individual cases. I slid out into the corridor again and lighted a Tiparillo, watching the courtroom door.

There buying coffee was Judge Nacht. He beamed and waddled over to me.

"Hello, Fitz," he smiled aimiably. "Lunch today?"

"I might be over," I said. "Say, Judge, could you do me a favor?"

"For the press—anything."

"A friend of mine has been reassigned—a court clerk—and I can't locate him. Could you help?"

For a magician, nothing could be easier. Judge Nacht beamed. He waddled to a phone booth, made two calls and came back with a telephone number for Al Wagner, who was now toiling in the distant pits of Brooklyn Civil Court. I would never have located him.

"Hello, Al? It's Ed Fitzgerald. I've got your opera tickets."

"Listen, you got me in trouble."

"I'm sorry, Al. You might as well get your tickets, though."

Silence.

"Five tickets. *Pagliacci.* Luciano Pavarotti."

I heard a faint groan. "What do you want?"

"Could you just find out when the Amster Case is on again in Manhattan Surrogate's Court?"

"I told you before. It's on for today."

"It's been postponed again until the twenty-sixth, I think. I need to know for sure."

"Mail me the tickets. I'll call you back."

So much for big shot Weinberg's attempt to freeze me out. There's more than one way to skin a cat.

Within a few minutes, the pay phone rang and Wagner was back on the line, saying that the Amster Case, as he had told me, was on for today.

"It was postponed, I tell you."

"Why won't people listen?" Wagner whined. "I told you it was on for today. Well, it was on and it's settled."

I almost dropped the phone.

"What do you mean, settled?"

"It was returned to the calendar and disposed of. There was no opposition to the petitioner's claim, so the estate was settled."

"You mean it's all over?"

"Yes. The case is closed."

"Well, what happened? Who was there? How much did she get?"

"I really don't know, Ted. I watched it for you. You should have been in court."

27.

I had been sitting out in the Atlantic Ocean in a life raft waiting for a ship to come along and pick me up, and it had passed me by in the middle of the night. Disposed of? There went my contradiction. Now the Reverend Schuyler would get his $500,000 altar and everyone would be happy. Weinberg, Maria and the judge were gathering up the Amster millions with all due legality right under my nose, and the cops would explain the Sanford Pearl murder away by arresting Tony Faso. There I would be trying to explain where I got that $500 and why I gave it away to Leeta Kane and Marcia Pearl.

Belinda's wrist turned red and then white where my hand clamped on it as I dragged her from Landlord and Tenant Court. She was protesting with little "What? What? What?s" as I pulled her out into the court corridor, but I was no longer in the mood for games.

"You got to Weinberg, didn't you?"

Another bewildered "What?"

"You told Weinberg I was here with you in Landlord and Tenant Court, didn't you?"

"What are you talking about?"

"You know what I'm talking about! You told him I was here, didn't you?"

"Yes. Yes I did. Why?"

What a wonderful plan I had worked out. There was no way the Amster estate could be settled without the presence in court of Maria/Belinda Amster herself. Of course not. But that was only in a proper, legal proceeding. In this con game, I had forgotten that Weinberg and Belinda had the judge in on it, too. When the judge is part of it, you can do anything.

"What's the matter?" Belinda was saying, searching my face in a fine show of bewildered concern.

"Stop it," I snapped. "Stop playing games, Maria!"

"What did you call me?"

"All he had to know was that I was safely out of the way, and they put the damned case on the calendar and rammed it through."

"What are you talking about, Ed?"

She was still watching me in hesitant confusion when I left and headed across through Foley Square, between the courthouses and to the New York Press parking zone behind Police Headquarters. I drove the Pinto up the F.D.R. Drive toward the office and my head was turning like the Wonder Wheel at Coney Island. In the middle of the giant ferris wheel loomed the face of Leonard the super in my building on East 82nd Street. Leonard is one of these people who drives me up the wall without even trying. You know how it is when somebody just aggravates you by the way they turn on a light switch? Leonard is fond of saying, "If it don't work, try it backwards." Idiotic. He'll be fixing a lamp or a sink drain and if things won't work he goes through his crazy reverse technique. My mind was doing a Leonard on me. Here was a two hundred million dollar estate in Surrogate's Court being settled, a coup that any lawyer would be ecstatic about and who would call a breast-beating press conference so he and Maria could be on the front page and the six o'clock news on TV.

If a lawyer were willing to pay anybody to get a story into the news, this was a prime candidate. And yet, Sandy Pearl had written nothing, and Bernie Weinberg was not out drumming up news stories about it. He hadn't even mentioned it to me or Harry Reeves or Jed Starnes. In fact, every effort had been made to assure that the case would never come to public attention or be mentioned anywhere. Even the papers had been sealed by a cooperative judge. The fact that there were no recent mentions of Weinberg in Sandy Pearl's stories made sense now, because he had not wanted anyone to write about the Amster Case or to even realize it was being disposed of. It was burglary by silence, grand larceny by stealth.

Applying Leonard the super's axiom, I looked at the whole thing in reverse. Finally, it made sense. Sandy Pearl wasn't being paid off to write about the Amster Case. He was being paid off *not* to. Maria Amster was bringing him those $100 bills because she and Weinberg knew that her claim to the money could not withstand any kind of public scrutiny.

Wonderful. Now that they had gotten away with it, I was figuring it out. And it still wasn't all clear. Sandy Pearl found out about the estate, and must have started to write something. He was persuaded not to write anything by those $500 payoffs from Maria Amster. But then he was murdered. What had gone wrong?

When I came off the elevator on the seventh floor I had the sensation of people telling everybody in waves that I was there. I kept hearing the announcement being repeated and repeated like a messenger preceding me. "He's here . . . he's here . . . there he is!"

By the time I got to the city desk, Ironhead Matthews was standing up red-faced and with a contorted mouth. He was saying something to me but I couldn't make it out at first.

"What?"

"I said thanks for putting in an appearance."

"He's getting away with it, Ironhead."

"Who?"

"Weinberg."

"Why weren't you at the D.A.'s office? Kirkman's

getting you cited for contempt and is swearing out a bench warrant for your arrest."

"I wasn't ready yet."

"Isn't that sweet? Where were you?"

"Landlord and Tenant Court."

Ironhead ran that through his inflamed brain and couldn't seem to find a place for it. "Landlord and Tenant Court?" He shook his head like a dog. "Landlord and Tenant Court?" He looked away, searching a subway map on the wall for an answer. "What does that have to do with this?"

"I'm telling you—while I was snookered in Landlord and Tenant Court, Weinberg and the judge put that damned estate back on the calendar in Surrogate's Court and rammed it through. I told Corcoran all about it. Goddammit, Weinberg's getting away with a couple of hundred million dollars and nobody will listen to me."

"How can anybody listen to you when you aren't there?" Ironhead raged. "Why didn't you come to 155 Leonard Street and tell it to the district attorney?"

"Ironhead," I said as calmly as I could, "how can I tell the district attorney that a judge and a lawyer pulled three murders so they could steal two hundred million dollars? And what about the minister?"

Ironhead's mouth worked and his eyes seemed to be in orbit around their sockets, like an animated Tom and Jerry cartoon character who had just been hit with a giant wooden mallet.

"Minister?"

"Yeah. I think he's just casting his bread upon the waters and doesn't really know what it's all about."

Ironhead seemed to be calculating things, adding up disasters in his mind, all the while chewing on his cigar, and keeping a migraine headache type of glare clamped on me. Charles W. Corcoran, the *Daily Trib* lawyer, was on his way from the D.A.'s office to the city room, and when he got there we would figure out what to do. Ironhead thought the best plan would be for me to "surrender" myself to Kirkman before things got any more tangled up. It sounded like I would be tossed into some cell somewhere and they would throw the key away. I was banished to my old rewrite desk to await Corcoran's arrival, by which time it was expected that I would "start making sense."

When I sat down, I noticed a manila envelope on my desk. My name was scrawled across it.

I opened the envelope and inside was a photograph of Bernard Weinberg walking into Surrogate's Court with a striking brunette. I got up and walked over to the picture desk.

"Hey, Pete," I said. "Who's the broad in the photo that was left on my desk?"

Pete looked up and took the photograph from my hands.

"You wanted a photog at Surrogate's Court this morning. By the way, where were you? Kenny said he couldn't find you."

I looked at the photograph. Weinberg, looking startled, walking with a flashy-looking brunette.

"That's Maria Amster?"

"Amster," said Pete. "Right."

I looked at the picture in confusion. It wasn't Belinda.

28.

"I forgot to call off the photog," I muttered.

"You didn't want it?" complained Pete.

"Oh, yes! Did I! It just blows my mind."

I went back to my desk with the photograph and stared at the image of Maria Amster. Brunette hair coiffed around her pretty head to frame a face that was all doe eyes and red mouth. A dress suitable for a fashion show, not a day in court. A slit in her skirt revealed a shapely leg. And she was wearing those shoes that are nothing but black strings.

The photograph had the effect on me of being hit with a bucket of cold water, or a pinch as in, "Pinch me so I'll know I'm not dreaming."

No wonder Belinda had looked at me in bewilderment. And what could I possibly say to her again? Where did she belong in all this, anyway?

There was the real Maria Amster, and there was Bernard Weinberg. And I knew that at last I'd found the stylish woman who had delivered those hundred-dollar bills to Sandy Pearl. There they were, walking around free with two hundred million and plans to go to Europe. One stop would be Switzerland and the Banque de Suisse Nationale in Geneva, I had no doubt. I realized something else, too. From the way Weinberg was holding Maria's arm, it wasn't only her money he coveted.

The couple in the photograph were not merely lawyer and client about to rob a dead man; they were love birds headed for a long and lavish honeymoon.

"Ironhead," I blurted, "it's not Belinda!"

"Belinda? Who's Belinda?"

"It's Maria Amster," I babbled somewhat breathlessly. "Dammit, why didn't I go to Surrogate's Court?"

"You weren't supposed to," he said, working up to another raving fit. "You were supposed to go where we could find you. A person is supposed to be at home or at work so somebody can find him."

"At work?" I said. "You know, I never tried him at work."

In another minute, I had Peggy on the phone, putting through a call to Reverend Schuyler in Topeka, Kansas.

"Hello, Reverend. Fitzgerald here—New York."

"Well, hello."

"Say, listen, Reverend, I've got good news. That money ought to be released pretty soon."

"Was the estate settled up there?"

"More or less. I'm just putting the story together now. Say, Reverend, I forgot to ask you where Roscoe Schaaf works."

"Roscoe? Oh, Mrs. Taylor's friend?"

"Yes."

"Why, he sells roofing and siding for that place over on Hudson Avenue."

"What company is that?"

"Let's see now, it's the Schnellbacher's. Schnellbacher's Roofing and Siding. Let me get you the number."

In a moment the reverend was back on the line with the Topeka number of Schnellbacher's Roofing, and a few minutes later I was talking to the general manager, Art Schnellbacher.

"Who do you want?"

"Roscoe Schaaf."

"You do, huh?" He made a disgusted noise. "Well, so do I. And a lot of other people."

"Why is that?"

"Roscoe has been a bad boy. He skipped town owing a

lot of people money. Including me. I happen to be his uncle, which is my misfortune. What do you want him for?"

I tried to think fast. "Well, I'm looking for him for a collection agency. Maybe we can help get some of that money back for you."

Roscoe's uncle snorted. "Fat chance. Roscoe and money can't seem to stick together."

"Would you know where he is?"

"Well, hell, he's with Mickey Taylor, naturally."

"Who?"

"Maria Taylor. Sam Taylor's ex. He took up with her and nothing has been able to hold him since. He's up there in New York City with her right now."

Roscoe was in the Big Apple with Maria? Well, well, well.

"Do you know where he's staying?"

"Last I heard it was the Wilton Hotel."

"Thanks."

"That's okay. Good luck. If you find him, tell him not to come back out here. The Shawnee County sheriff's got out a warrant for him on those bum checks."

I hung up the phone and felt like shouting. Roscoe Schaaf was here with Maria. Wasn't that lovely?

Down to my Pinto. Clickety-clickety across town to Eighth Avenue and north to Columbus Circle at Central Park, where I left the Pumpkin in a NYP zone.

The Wilton Hotel was one of those residental hotels on West 58th Street near Central Park with a big, impressive green canopy over the front door, a doorman dressed like the leader of the Marine Corps band, and a cavernous, gloomy lobby. It had seen better days, but was still in fairly good shape.

"You have a Roscoe Schaaf registered?"

"Roscoe Schaaf?" The desk clerk smiled and checked. He kept saying the name to himself softly as though making sure he wouldn't forget it. "Roscoe Schaaf . . . Roscoe . . . here we are. Four-twelve."

I got on the house phone and called Roscoe's room. It rang and rang and rang. Roscoe, it seemed, wasted little time at home, whether he was in Topeka or on the road.

Off the lobby to one side was a tiny cocktail lounge that was even gloomier than the lobby. I could watch the elevator from there, so I strolled over and went in. The bar was a three-sided nook that stuck out of the wall with three bar stools on each side.

"Schaefer."

The bartender put a beer in front of me, and I squinted into the afternoon darkness of the place. When my eyes got accustomed to the half-light, I realized there was somebody else already sitting at the corner of the bar against the wall. A tall, handsome guy in a brown plaid sports jacket with a tanned, open, country club face. Beside him sat a trim brunette with an alert head that was bobbing around like a robin searching a lawn for a worm. While I was focusing on her in the dim light, she suddenly got up and walked right past me and out into the lobby. I almost spoke to her as she went past, but she was too quick for me, and when I looked around out into the lobby she was hurrying to grab a man and hug and kiss him. She almost had to bend down to kiss the pasty, smiling parchment face.

I couldn't hear what they were saying, but Weinberg's dry little laugh reached me, and Maria's high tinkling. She kept her arm around him, and he held her possessively as they walked into an elevator and the doors closed.

I slid off the bar stool and went to the servile hotel desk clerk. "Do you have a Maria Amster registered?" He checked but there was no Maria Amster.

"Oh, yes," I said. "Her married name is Taylor."

"Taylor," he chirped. "Oh, yes. Mrs. Sam Taylor. Four-ten."

Maria from Kansas was in four-ten and Roscoe Schaaf from Kansas was in four-twelve. How convenient. I went back to the bar and sipped my Schaefer. The smiling country club face was still sitting in the corner.

"Well, I guess I'll just have another," he said to the bartender. The accent was nothing you'd hear in Brooklyn or the Bronx. I'd never been in Kansas, but I knew it was right out of the wheat fields.

"Been in New York long?" I opened.

Western accent turned and smiled amiably. "Couple weeks," he said. "Big place."

"Where you from?"

"Kansas. Topeka, Kansas. That's the capital, you know."

"Never would have guessed."

Country club face smiled and laughed. "Don't guess I can pass for a New Yorker, can I?" He picked up his drink, which was a double Scotch, and gulped at it. I moved over next to him and lighted a Tiparillo.

"Listen, I could sit here and play cat and mouse with you, Roscoe, but I haven't got the time."

Country club face gave me a startled look. "You know me?"

"Roscoe Schaaf. Topeka, Kansas. Roofing and siding salesman. Your uncle's looking for you."

"Who you with?"

Good question. I deputized myself. "Sheriff's office."

Roscoe turned a surprised face on me. "They got a sheriff here in New York?"

"Sure have, Roscoe. We don't ride horses, but we can serve arrest warrants from Shawnee County."

In my years as a reporter, almost nobody ever asked to see my press card, so I figured Roscoe wouldn't ask to see a deputy sheriff's badge. It's a routine practice for reporters to pass themselves off as police sergeants or even inspectors to question people who might not otherwise give an ink-stained wretch the time of day. Actually, I had only found out where the sheriff's office was located a few days earlier when a sign in the lobby of the Surrogate's Court building caught my eye. It was in the same building down on Chambers Street.

A ton of hay landed on Roscoe. He shook his head. He apparently was familiar with the Shawnee County sheriff's office. He lighted a long, white cigarette and exhaled a cloud of blue smoke.

"What's your name, anyhow?"

"Harry Reeves."

"Well, listen Harry, I can get all the money I owe by tomorrow morning."

"Look, Roscoe, I believe you," I said. "Really. You look like a nice guy to me. But your uncle Art, he's pretty ticked off. And I've got a warrant I got to execute."

"If I gave you the cash, couldn't you call the sheriff out there and my uncle Art and tell them I've made it good? I bet we could get the charges dropped and this whole thing wrapped up."

Roscoe was a pretty good talker, at that. I sat silently, as though considering.

"I'll be able to get the money at about five o'clock."

"Five?"

"I'm coming into some money."

"From whom?"

"I can't tell you that."

There we sat, chatting politely, and I suddenly realized that the Amster estate papers would be signed in Judge Foley's chambers in less than half an hour. Even as the thought flashed through my mind, I saw Weinberg and Maria come out of the elevator and cross the lobby on the way out of the hotel.

167

"Okay, Roscoe," I rushed, lurching to my feet. "I'm sorry, but I'm taking you in!"

"But I thought we had a deal," Roscoe groaned.

"Got to clear it with the sheriff."

"But we can settle it ourselves if you'll just wait till six o'clock."

Waiting until six o'clock was the one thing I couldn't do.

"Sorry, Roscoe," I said, hurrying him out of the bar. "All warrants got to be cleared by five o'clock. The sheriff's got a rule."

"I never heard a rule like that," Roscoe grumbled as he came out through the lobby.

Neither had the sheriff.

As we came outside, Weinberg's limousine was rolling away down the street.

29.

I hailed a yellow cab to take us downtown. I didn't dare walk him to my pumpkin Pinto over at Columbus Circle, because while he might buy the suggestion that my NYP license plates stood for New York Police, as some people think, he also might realize I was a phony.

"Where to?" the cabbie said.

"Foley Square."

"Art's gonna regret this," Roscoe muttered. "I'm gonna pay him back for this. Shit fire, am I gonna pay him back."

I let Roscoe stew as we bumped along southward while I tried to think. By the time the cab was approaching the World Trade Center towers in lower Manhattan, he looked as shriveled up and miserable as something on a tray at the Fulton Fish Market. I was in as much distress, because I didn't want to reach the sheriff's office any more than he did.

"I'm not out to get you, Roscoe. Can you give me some kind of assurance? Where are you getting the money?"

Roscoe found some hint of softening in my words, and he sat forward. "It's an inheritance," he said.

"You're inheriting money today?"

"It's the same thing, Harry. My girl friend."

"Is she the one I saw in the lobby with that man?"

"That's the lawyer," Roscoe said.

"She seemed pretty friendly with him."

"Friendly? With that old fool?" Roscoe laughed. "That's just for show."

"Whereabouts on Foley Square?" the cabbie inquired.

"Thirty-one Chambers Street."

He swung left across Chambers and we went by City Hall

Park and the old Tweed Courthouse to Surrogate's Court. As we drove up, Weinberg's long, black limousine with the BW license plate was parked in front of the courthouse. We got out and I paid the driver, watching Roscoe out of the corner of my eye. He was looking at Weinberg's limo.

"What building is this?"

"Sheriff's office," I said.

"Looks like a courthouse. Look at all the statues on the roof."

"Well, sure, it is a courthouse. You get so used to it being the sheriff's office. This is Surrogate's Court."

"This is where Mickey is."

"Oh, yeah?"

"She's right upstairs in Judge Foley's chambers signing to get that money."

I led him slowly into the lobby under the Egyptian cat gods and between the perched black eagles, wanting to give Weinberg and Maria enough time to go up in the elevator. In the gloomy marble nave beyond the lobby, they were nowhere in sight. Courthouse employees were streaming out as we went in. City employees are like that. At four-thirty you can get trampled if you're near an exit, and by five o'clock public buildings are like the deserted ruins of Pompeii.

I walked Roscoe to the elevator, and my mind was spinning like one of those whirling, tilting rides at Coney Island. Roscoe was docilely allowing me to take him right to the sheriff's office, and then what would I do? He needed a destination that would jolt him.

"Maybe you'll get a chance to say goodbye, since she's right here in the building," I said. The elevator swayed slowly upward.

"What do you mean, goodbye?" Roscoe said, his eyes searching my face.

"Well, we've got to get out to Kennedy Airport and get a

170

plane to Kansas. I don't know if we can fly direct, or if we'll have to go through Kansas City.''

Roscoe backed away until he bumped the elevator wall. ''Kansas?''

''We just got to get you arraigned and clear the warrant by five, and we'll be on our way,'' I said casually.

Roscoe surged toward me, suddenly all in a dither, squaring around anxiously to face me like Billy Martin baiting an umpire. ''Hey, I can't go back to Kansas! Jesus, what are you talking about?''

''Roscoe, I got a warrant for your arrest.''

''I didn't know you were taking me to Kansas.''

''It's a Kansas warrant.''

The enormity of his trouble was finally getting to him. ''I didn't think it was so urgent.'' He stood there poleaxed.

''I got to get some handcuffs,'' I said.

''I can't go to Kansas,'' he blurted. ''I'm going to Hawaii tomorrow on my honeymoon.''

Honeymoon? That little piece of information hit me right between the eyes. That was the message Roscoe had to deliver to Weinberg in Judge Foley's chambers.

''Well, I'm sorry, Roscoe. I really am.''

Roscoe checked his watch. I checked mine, too. It was ten to five. ''It's only ten minutes to five,'' he said. ''Couldn't you give me those ten minutes?''

''Well, hell, what can you do in ten minutes?''

''I can get the money. I know I can.''

The elevator shuddered to a halt on six, and I led Roscoe out into the marble hallway in front of the sheriff's office. Two huge barred gates in tasteful bronze rose almost to the ceiling in corridors leading off to both sides, and dead ahead was the sheriff's office. It was as far as I could go, because the New York County sheriff wouldn't know what the hell to do with a criminal arrest warrant even if I had one to give him.

The sheriff enforces civil judgments and evicts people.

"If you could go on into the judge's chambers and get this straightened out right away," I said, "I might be able to stall for another fifteen to twenty minutes. But you got to go in there and get a certified check with somebody's name on it besides yours."

"I will," Roscoe said anxiously.

"Can you get that lawyer to co-sign it?"

"I'll get somebody to. Don't worry."

Roscoe was straining back toward the elevator doors, away from the big "Sheriff's Office" sign, but I kept my hand on his sleeve.

"I'll be down in a few minutes. Now don't make a sucker out of me, Roscoe."

"Don't worry," he promised, and lunged into the elevator.

The second he disappeared, I jumped into the sheriff's office and asked if I could use a phone.

"Hello, Danny? Give me Ironhead right away!"

Danny seemed to almost choke on that. "You *want* Ironhead?"

"Yes. Right now."

"Okay. He's been screaming for you."

Ironhead came snarling onto the phone. "I don't believe it. I actually got you. Where are you? I told you not to leave the city room."

"Ironhead, listen—I'm on top of the whole thing. I've got Roscoe."

"Roscoe? Who the hell is Roscoe?"

"Maria's boy friend. And get this—they're married!"

"Is that so? Well, now that *is* a big scoop. Why do I keep asking you questions?" He sounded perplexed and out of patience. "You give me answers but you don't tell me anything. Get your ass back up here."

"But I can't now, Ironhead."

172

"You *what?*"

"This thing is ready to break."

"Fitzgerald, I want a simple answer to a simple question. Ready? Where are you?"

"At Surrogate's Court."

"I'm now going to ask you a second simple question. Ready? *Why?*"

"Because this whole damn thing is ready to happen in Judge Foley's chambers."

"I checked with the Newspaper Guild. I can't fire you without a stupid hearing, see, and I'm not spending any more time on you."

"But I've got the story now!"

"You will report to Brooklyn to the press shack at midnight. You will remain on Brooklyn night police forever—or until you have reported to Manhattan Assistant District Attorney Edward Kirkman. If he doesn't arrest you first. Is that clear?"

"You're making a mistake, Ironhead."

"I made a mistake the day I let your dopey-looking puss into my city room!"

Blam. Errrrrrrrrgh . . .

That's what I get for trying to get an exclusive.

30.

I wish I could tell you that Brooklyn night police was something I could just bravely tough out. But it wasn't. I had worked enough midnight-to-eight lobster tricks when I first started out. I just had to hope that if I could come up with the Amster story, Ironhead might relent. Although Ironhead has never been one of your champion relenters.

I slipped down the marble stairway to the mezzanine floor between six and five, where a door opens onto the balcony of Judge Foley's courtroom. They don't use the balcony anymore, so I thought I could slip in unnoticed. The gloomy, cavernous, wood-paneled courtroom was deserted but from somewhere below muffled voices floated up. Carefully down the wide, wooden staircase that would have done justice to the one at Tara in *Gone With the Wind*. Past the marble fireplace and under the three crystal chandeliers.

Off one end of the courtroom were padded swinging doors. I leaned on one enough to get a look through into another hallway. Through that door another frosted glass door was visible. I walked up to it and voices floated through quite clearly.

"Is everything ready?" Weinberg said.

"Yes. It only has to be signed."

"Wonderful." A satisfied purr from Weinberg. "So you see, Maria, it's done."

A happy and relieved tinkle of laughter from Mickey Amster. I could imagine the red-mouth smile on her pretty face.

"Mrs. Amster, you sign in three places," the judge said. "There . . . there . . . and there."

"All right."

Papers ruffled as pages were turned.

"Can I draw money out yet?" said Maria.

"I'll take care of that," the purring cat said smoothly.

"Do I understand that congratulations are in order for you two?" the judge said and laughed softly.

Then Weinberg laughed.

Maria let out a brief little giggle.

A door opened somewhere and closed.

"What's that?" said Weinberg.

Judge Foley called out, "Hello? Is that you, Mrs. Nealy?"

Another door opened and I heard the friendly Elks Club voice of Roscoe.

"Judge Foley? Oh, there you are Mickey."

"May I help you?" the judge's cultured business voice said. "Who are you looking for?"

"I'm looking for Maria," said Roscoe, and then in a rush, "Mickey, I'm in trouble!"

"What are you doing here?" An annoyed, hushed gasp.

"You know this man?" From Weinberg.

"Roscoe, what is it?"

"Mickey, dammit, I've got to have some money right away."

"What?"

"I mean this second! Or they're taking me back to Kansas."

"What are you talking about?"

"Who is this? Who are you? I represent Mrs. Amster here. What's this all about?"

"Listen, Weinberg, if this is all settled, I want to talk to Mickey."

The lawyer's voice rose, like a wind beginning to build to a gust, much as it did in divorce court when he had to shout over the objections of Mickey Silberman. "You seem to know me—but I don't know you!"

"It's all right, Bernie," Maria interrupted, her tinkle

gone into a nervous trill. "I'll talk to him in the other room."

"No, it's *not* all right." The rising wind was still gathering velocity. "Who is this person and what is he doing here? Who are you?"

"Roscoe Schaaf. Don't worry about it. Mickey—I need five thousand in cash right now!"

"Roscoe, you shouldn't have come barging in here like this."

"Goddammit, they're going to arrest me."

"Roscoe—is that your name, Roscoe?—would you mind telling me your connection with my client?"

"It's all right, Bernard. He's a friend."

"He seems to think he's more than a friend," said Weinberg.

"Listen, I'd like to play along like this, but I'm in a helluva jam," said Roscoe, a note of desperation edging into his western twang. "You'll get your fee, Weinberg."

"My fee?"

I was devastated not to be on the other side of the frosted glass door to see if that parchment-paper face went even paler or if it possibly flushed with anger.

"Roscoe, we'll talk later."

"Goddammit, the sheriff is here to take me back to Kansas," Roscoe raved. "Don't you understand what I'm saying? How the hell are we going to Hawaii tomorrow if that goddamn deputy busts me?"

"Roscoe, will you shut up! Oh, you idiot!" Maria spit·it out and I had to imagine the unhappiness on Weinberg's pale face.

"Hawaii?"

There was a silence.

"Hawaii? Maria, what is he talking about? Roscoe, what's this about Hawaii?"

"I said you'd get your fee."

"Maria?"

No answer.

"Haven't you told him about us?"

No answer.

"Maria?"

Finally Roscoe jumped in again. "For god's sake, Weinberg, what's the matter with you?"

"I don't follow you. Perhaps you could tell me," said Weinberg, and I had a feeling that dot of rage was shimmering in the deep recesses of his eyes.

"I might as well tell him, Mickey. Mickey?"

Maria apparently had lost her voice.

"Mickey's my wife."

After a moment, Weinberg's voice came again, controlled but tense. "Your wife? Maria is your wife? Maria, is this true? Maria?"

"Yes."

A long breath exhaled. "It seems I've been acting the fool here, doesn't it?" A dry, malicious laugh, self-mocking and with a flat edge of sarcasm.

"Roscoe, you idiot." Mickey's words were weak, filled with apprehension.

"I couldn't help it, Mickey. He'll get his fee. A deputy sheriff is coming up here to arrest me if I don't cover those checks back in Topeka."

"What's your name—Roscoe what?"

"Roscoe Schaaf."

"Well, Mr. Schaaf, I'm afraid you have a profound misconception about this entire transaction."

"Bernie, I'm sorry," Maria began. "I tried to tell you not to get serious. I never dreamed you really could have imagined . . . I was shocked when you talked about it."

"Did you hear that, Herb?" said Weinberg levelly, and I had to believe the molten core of his eyes were blue flames of naked fury. "Maria never *dreamed* or *imagined* . . . all the way from Kansas. All these months. But somehow it never occurred to you to drop out of this little arrangement, did it?"

"Why should it? It's my family's money."

The laugh was still dry but it was downright malevolent now.

"Listen to that, Herb. She thinks she can talk to me like some snooty little clerk. Is that what you think, Maria?"

"Bernard . . ."

"Don't you call me Bernard!"

"Bernie," the judge interceded. "Take it easy."

"Take it easy?" Weinberg's voice was stretched like a tight wire. "Smart little hicks from Kansas. So you think you'll pay my fee, do you? And what do you suppose that would be?"

"I don't know," said Roscoe. "Anything you say."

"All of it?"

"What?"

"All of it. That's what I say."

Roscoe laughed uncertainly. "Anything reasonable, I mean."

"Calm down, Bernie," the judge said.

"This whole thing was mine," said Weinberg. "I didn't need you, Maria. I worked on this for years. Once Herb told me about it, I did the rest. I decided to let you in on a good thing because . . . well, never mind. I could have picked any little waitress in Brooklyn. There's no fool like an old fool, is there?"

"I don't get this," came the ingenuous Kansas twang.

"You think you're going to get a piece of this now? Do you actually think I'm some hayseed clodhopper?" He laughed a little. "People are amazing. Never satisfied. They want more than they're worth. Just like that pushy little reporter. You know about that little reporter, don't you, Maria? He was doing all right for doing nothing, but he had to have an equal share, too. Like you, Roscoe. Did you tell Roscoe what happened to that blackmailing reporter, Maria?"

"No."

"What happened?" asked Roscoe.

"He died of greed," said Weinberg. "He was only supposed to be given a scare, but these things don't always work out exactly."

"Bernie, there's plenty for all," said Judge Foley.

"Not any more. There was, I thought. Half and half for you and me, Herb. You see, Maria, I assumed my half would be yours and mine. You would have been a very rich woman. But everybody who hears about this wants in. Now there's Roscoe."

"You should have stayed back at the hotel, Roscoe," Maria whined. "I told you to stay put."

"I told you—a deputy sheriff is coming up here any minute."

"What is this deputy sheriff business?" said Weinberg. "A deputy sheriff from Kansas?"

"No, no, goddammit! A New York deputy."

"A what?"

"Yes. He brought me right here to the sheriff's office upstairs, and said he'd give me a few minutes to come down here and get enough money to clear up his warrant."

Weinberg and Foley both started talking at once, because the words became jumbled and highly charged. Somebody wanted to know what deputy sheriff, and somebody else wanted to know what he meant that the deputy was there in the building.

"Hell, he almost dragged me right into the sheriff's office on the sixth floor," said Roscoe.

There was a silence, and then Weinberg spoke up. "The sheriff's office on the sixth floor? Don't be ridiculous. The sheriff wouldn't execute an arrest warrant."

"He did, I tell you."

"What did he look like?"

"Well, he was kind of rumpled looking. Average size. Just an ordinary-looking guy, like any deputy sheriff."

Nothing like hearing somebody give a glowing description of you.

"Did he show you any identification?"

"No."

"Who could it be?" Weinberg asked.

"Oh, good god," said the judge.

"What's wrong?" asked Roscoe.

"That was no deputy sheriff," said Weinberg. "I don't know who it was, but it wasn't a deputy. If he didn't show any identification, it probably wasn't a police officer either."

Well, it didn't take Weinberg the lawyer and Foley the judge long to compare notes about who had been snooping around asking questions about the estate. Once the judge mentioned that Fitzgerald the nosy reporter had been up to see him, Weinberg pounced on it immediately. It was fascinating to hear them figure out that the deputy was me.

But it was a little less fascinating when Weinberg used some legal projection.

"If he went through all that to get Roscoe up here, he's got to be here someplace listening to us," said Weinberg.

And that's where I started backpedaling slowly away from the frosted door toward the wooden doors leading to the courtroom. I also knew what happened to pushy reporters. I stopped tiptoeing when Roscoe's astonished voice reached me.

"Hey" he said suddenly, his voice an octave higher than before, "Jesus, what are you doing with that gun?"

"Shut up! Find that goddam deputy sheriff, you damned fool! He's a newspaper reporter!"

"A what?"

"Oh, my god," said Maria.

"Bernie, you can't do that," moaned the terrified judge.

"We can't let him get out of here," said Weinberg, and the frosted door from the judge's chambers flung open. Through the door strode the diminutive lawyer with a silver gun in his hand. I dived through the doors into the court-room as Weinberg shouted, "Come back here!"

The first slug ripped a slash a foot long in the leather that covered the padded, swinging door. I didn't so much hear it as smell the sharp stench of gunpowder.

Into the dark courtroom and scramble up the wooden staircase to the balcony.

The swinging doors opened and closed.

BLAM! An echo crashed against the walls and ceiling and bounced back again, and crashed out again, like a berserk accordion of sound.

Through the door on the balcony to the mezzanine hall-way. Beat it down the marble flight of stairs, wondering about trying the elevator. If I did, he might be on it. If I didn't he might beat me to the lobby.

Pound down the stairs, breathing hard, my feet making so much clattering on the marble that I thought I must be heard all the way to the Battery.

When I reached the elaborate, marble main stairway lead-ing from the lobby balcony to the great floor of the nave, there was a stillness and an emptiness in the place suitable to its tomblike structure. Dim, late afternoon light filtered through the curved glass skylight that vaulted the ceiling of the vast enclosure. I saw no signs of life, and the silence was a challenge to any movement on the marble steps.

Down the marble stairs slowly.

BLAM!

Crescendoing echoes. A zinging flash of light ripping against the marble balustrade and pinging off one marble wall and then another like a deadly projectile in a game of electronic Ping-Pong. The place was a horror for ricochets, all marble surfaces that sent the slug whistling madly in geometric slanting darts of fire.

"Give it up, Weinberg!"

"All I need is you." The disembodied voice echoed boomingly so that I couldn't locate him.

"And Roscoe and Maria."

"No, no. Roscoe can be handled. And Maria. My only problem is you."

BLAM! A flash of fire from the black eagle perched in the lobby. He was camped at the front door. The only way out.

I wish I could tell you that I threw my copy pencil in the gloom and struck him in the eye with it and carried him back to Ironhead in a laundry bag. But the next thing I knew, the Chambers Street doors were opening, and Weinberg dashed from the lobby across the marble main floor nave and halfway up the marble staircase across from the one I was sprawled on.

Shapes came flooding into the courthouse.

"Police!"

And then all hell broke loose. Bullets were crashing all over the area, zinging off the walls and floor. Flood lights came on. Two or three loudspeakers blared into the place, drowning each other out. I lay flat out on a marble step and tried to stick my face into the stone.

When the shooting stopped, shapes moved in along with the spotlights.

"Hey," I shouted. "It's me—Fitzgerald. I'm coming out!"

"Stay put!"

But I wasn't about to lie there in that goddam shooting gallery. Down the steps, slither and dive out into the sungod lobby.

The Steadman Brothers.

Behind them, uniformed cops from Emergency Service.

"Who's in there?" said Detective Henderson.

"Bernard Weinberg."

"The lawyer?"

"The lawyer."

"What the hell's he doing?"

"Trying to shoot me."

"Why?"

"It's a long story, Steadman."

A cop got out an electric bullhorn and told whoever it was to come out with his hands up. Nothing. Then Henderson called Weinberg by name.

"Come on out, Weinberg."

Nothing.

After a while, the cops went in and found Bernard Weinberg crouched on the marble stairway with a bullet in his head. It was a .22 caliber slug.

31.

I wound up sharing the by-line on the story with Dubbs Brewer, because of all the cops that cascaded into Surrogate's Court like the swarm of Thugs in *Gunga Din*. Corky Richards got a terrific photograph of Weinberg slumped down on the marble stairway with the .22 automatic cradled in both of his hands across his chest. There was a fine, dignified photo of Judge Foley from the files, showing him when he was appointed, because he wouldn't let us take a live shot of him; and a gray-faced, bewildered Roscoe Schaaf looked out of another photo like a Kansas heifer being led into the stockyards.

Maria got star billing, along with Weinberg, and smiled at the photogs as though she'd just signed a movie contract.

It was one of those long, stretched-out evenings when you are hauled this way and that by different people all demanding your immediate attention and angry at not being attended to first. Ironhead stood over me at my V.D.T. machine in the office as I wrote the damned story, and Dubbs Brewer leaned over and kept telling me to mention this or that detective, not to forget Lt. Dickson of Homicide and Inspector McCarthy and who-the-hell-knows-who-else.

"Come on, come on, get the goddam copy out," Ironhead hissed at me. "Why the hell didn't you tell me about all this? Shut up and write. Next time, talk to your city editor! What a pisser of a story! Stop dawdling, you damn hoople."

Every time I finished three or four paragraphs, Ironhead would scream at me to send it through the electronic video display terminal to his machine. You push a button and the story slips off your video screen, blipping magically through the wires—or maybe through the air for all I know—and when Ironhead pushes a button on his V.D.T. at the city desk, the story pops onto his screen. Don't ask me how it works. Anyway, only after I'd sent him a few paragraphs was there time to take a glance around for a second. There was Assistant District Attorney Edward Kirkman standing sour-faced with the managing editor and nervous Charles W. Corcoran, the *Daily Trib* lawyer, all looking very grim and dour and impatient. Then there was this Ralph Nader-looking gray suit person from the Temporary State Commission on Judicial Conduct who wanted to know why I hadn't told them about this case of possible judicial misconduct. Not to mention Lt. Dickson of Homicide, who was pacing back and forth in the picture department followed by his bodyguard Sergeant Hogan. I don't know who all else was lined up waiting to pat me on the back or chew me out, or both.

Well, finally the story was tapped into the electronic monster for the Four Star edition and I could sit back to light a Tiparillo. They came in waves then, so that I had to tell the whole, complicated, tenuous story from the top to the bottom about five different times.

Henderson and Singleton/Steadman were being interviewed by Kramie Marshall, our blonde and delicious feature writer, so I stepped over to them.

"I tried to call you guys, but couldn't find you," I told them. "How'd you happen to come to Surrogate's Court?"

"We were looking for ycu, too," said Henderson.

"What for?"

"To arrest you," said Steadman. "You're in contempt of court for not showing up at the D.A.'s office."

And I'm a son of a bitch if he didn't give me the summons right then and there while I was supposed to be a hero.

"Who told you where I was?" I grumbled, finding it

hard to believe that Ironhead would have given me away, despite his troglodyte screeching.

"Your lawyer, Corcoran," said Henderson.

"He's an officer of the court," Steadman explained.

It figured. Ironhead told Corcoran, and he told the D.A.'s office. Corcoran was one of these knee-jerk law types who did everything by the book, and I might have been really upset with him if his bungling hadn't saved my life.

The Great Estate Caper stayed in the news for quite a while after that. Maria Amster kept insisting that she really believed herself to be a distant relative of Sheldon Amster, and said she was shocked to learn that Weinberg apparently was trying to manipulate her.

She turned state's evidence and testified against Judge Foley, who on advice of counsel said not a word to anyone. Maria got a suspended sentence. Judge Herbert Foley pleaded *nolo contendere* and was allowed to retire quietly to Florida.

Roscoe Schaaf talked loudly, more or less expertly and at length to anyone who would listen, and became something of a Manhattan celebrity playboy as long as people would pay for the drinks. The only trouble was that Roscoe didn't really know what the hell it was all about.

You might not believe this, but I had to spend a night at the Brooklyn night police shack before I could get to see the D.A. and tell him everything. He didn't really need me by then, because it was all in the paper.

It turned out that Arny Hayes had owed money to Weinberg for defending him, and Kirkman concluded that the ballplayer was trying to discharge that debt when he pushed Sandy Pearl in front of a rented car driven by Weinberg. Whether Arny really pushed him or Sandy stumbled because of the knockout drops was never really determined.

As for Rita Faso, I was so hell-bent on finding the elusive index number that when I checked the case out in the Bronx

I forgot to ask who the lawyer was. Weinberg, naturally. Kirkman theorized that she, too, was paying Pasty-face's fee when she came around to spy on me.

"I figured all along she had to have been forced if she put the make on somebody like you," Reeves said when he heard about it.

Weinberg knew in advance I was trying to find Arny, and he got there first with his .22. The same with Rita. It seems John the information booth clerk told him I was looking for her.

I won't bother to tell you how long it took me to explain things to Belinda Sharpe. She wouldn't even talk to me for a while, and she started slipping back into a kind of numbness again. I kept explaining the tangled mess to her again and again, telling her I had cast her in the web through my own overactive imagination.

We finally concluded that Weinberg *was* using her to spy on me, but that she didn't realize there was anything sinister in his seemingly polite questions about me. She took his interest in her as that of an older, experienced lawyer extending professional courtesy toward a tyro launching into practice. After all, that's what Belinda would have done.

"But how could you imagine me with Bernard Weinberg?"

"Bee, I had run out of other possibilities."

"You're an idiot."

"Guilty."

She's over it all now, thank you, and launched as a trademark attorney. That was why she was hanging around the courts. It took so long to explain things that we spent quite a lot of time together, and we finally decided it was silly to have two apartments.

My place on East 82nd Street is a place of hope now. When we get home, she babbles on about her day in court, and I carry on about the latest craziness at the *Trib*.

As for the Sheldon Amster estate, all of a sudden a mob of fresh, new heirs are coming out of the woodwork and the State of New York is currently battling them for the money.

But Reeves and I are staying the hell out of that mess. We don't cover Surrogate's Court, and we don't want to be held responsible for it.

LAWRENCE SANDERS